Within the Walls of Hell

T0319128

Taniform Martin Wanki

Langaa Research & Publishing CIG
Mankon, Bamenda

Publisher

Langaa RPCIG
Langaa Research & Publishing Common Initiative Group
P.O. Box 902 Mankon
Bamenda
North West Region
Cameroon
Langaagrp@gmail.com
www.langaa-rpcig.net

Distributed in and outside N. America by African Books Collective
orders@africanbookscollective.com
www.africanbookcollective.com

ISBN: 9956-726-53-2

Dedication

I am highly indebted to Mr. Chi Emmanuel and Mrs. Chi Lum Sarah for being the best parents in the world. They gave me knowledge which is the best gift parents could give to their children.

I am also indebted to Achiri Fidelis whose contribution to my education is enormous.

Special thanks also go to my best friends in the world. I am thinking about Alangeh Linda, Mbom Peter, Shu Jerome, Dingha Pius, Nguefack Rachel, Madam Viban Florence, Madam Ayangwo Debora and Madam Chuyeh Maryanne

Characters

Messenger

Common Man

Act One

Scene 1: This scene opens with Sandi outside the tall Iron Gate. It opens and he walks in after the Messenger.

Messenger: (*Leads him to his room*)

Sandi: (*Follows the Messenger and enters the room shown him. The floor is bear with only a torn mat. There is a lot of heat and he feels thirsty. Goes to the tap at one corner of the room and turns it. It makes a noise but does not cough out water*). What is wrong with the tap? It's not flowing and I'm really thirsty.

Messenger: I noticed.

Sandi: So? Aren't you going to get me some water instead of standing there doing nothing? Is this how you treat your guests here?

Messenger: Did I hear you say 'guest'? As far as I know, you never received any invitation from anybody, did you?

Sandi: There I think you are right. I never received any invitation. In that case, I don't know what I'm doing here. So, I will just walk out that gate just the same way I walked in.

Messenger: (*smiles*) you are free to go. No one is stopping you.

Sandi: (*leaves messenger in the room and heads towards the gate. Gets to the gate. Tries to push it open but it doesn't open. Tries again with all his strength but it still does not open. Walks back to the room where he left the messenger*). The gate wouldn't open.

Messenger: I know that.

Sandi: (*surprise*) why don't you go and open it?

Messenger: I didn't lock it. You entered after me and the gate closed up on its own, right?

Sandi: (*In exasperation*) so, who is supposed to open the damn gate?

Messenger: (*very calmly*) the gate can only open to let someone in. It cannot open to let anyone out. Once you get in here, you can never get out again.

Sandi: And what about you? I met you outside the gate before we walked in here together. Does it mean you have never been in here before?

Messenger: I have but I am different. I can walk in and out because I'm a Messenger. My job is to clarify your doubts in case you feel that your presence in here is unjustified. Are you still thirsty?

Sandi: What a question! The heat is suffocating and I badly need water.

Messenger: You did not send us anything to prepare clean potable water for you here while you were down there. What you sowed down there is what you will reap here.

Sandi: (*looking so confused*) what do you mean?

Messenger: What I mean is that the kind of life you live in the world below your feet determines where you go thereafter. Did you live a good life while you were down there?

Sandi: I lived a good life.

Messenger: What makes you say that?

Sandi: I prayed many times a day and went to the house of prayer on weekdays and weekends too. I also did entirely what my spiritual leader told me to do.

Messenger: Saying your prayers regularly and going to the house of prayer was good. But I'm interested in what your spiritual leader told you to do. What did he tell you to do from the moment he became your spiritual leader?

Sandi: My spiritual leader told me that if I wanted to go to that place where all human beings dream of after death, I must die fighting for my religion or for a good course. He also added that dying for my religion would earn me the crown of a martyr in addition to eternal life. I was promised many virgins in the life beyond.

Messenger: Did you believe that every thing your spiritual leader asked you to do was right?

Sandi: (*without hesitating*). Yes I believed in everything he asked me to do. He told me and many others that our gaining eternal life depended on how we carried out his instructions to the latter.

Messenger: What did he ask you to do in order to be crowned a martyr and also gain eternal life?

Sandi (*Very enthusiastic*) First of all, he told us that we had to be the soldiers of our Creator by winning souls for our religion. He also added that anyone who refused to accept our religion was an infidel and instructed us in such a situation to give him or her a deadline to convert or face the consequences.

Messenger: That is interesting. But there is one word you used whose meaning I do not quite master. The word is 'Infidel'. Can you find a synonym which can make me understand?

Sandi: (*remains silent for a while searching through his brain to find an answer*) Yes, I think I've got it. A synonym could be 'Unfaithful'.

Messenger: That is wonderful. Now tell me, were those you call infidels unfaithful to you, your spiritual leader, Creator, or your religion?

Sandi: They were, to my religion and spiritual leader who was charged with leading everyone to the Creator.

Messenger: (*Smiles*) That was a very technical answer. But let me explain something to you. When you were down there and even right now there is still a saying that many roads lead to Rome, right?

6

Sandi: Right.

Messenger: In the same vein, many roads lead to our Creator. The road that leads to our Creator is called religion. But you are not supposed to concentrate on the road and forget your destination. You concentrated too much on the road which was your religion and forgot the destination which was our Creator. If you had taken up your head once in a while to look at your destination, perhaps you might have realized that the paths others took linked up with yours somewhere. However, if religions are the roads, it does not mean that all of the roads lead to our Creator. Take yours for example, did anybody who belonged to your religion visit the grave and return to tell you that it led to our Creator?

Sandi: No.

Messenger: In that case, you had no right to impose your religion or way of life on others who did not want to accept it; let alone calling them odd names. Once you cross that bar which marks the boundary between this world and the one you've just come from, you account for your deeds alone. No one becomes your mouth-piece. That means that salvation is personal. If you forced someone to do something right and the act was not coming from the heart of that person, then it was useless. My master is interested in what comes from the heart. No one is supposed to force another to get into the Land of Eternal Happiness or Paradise if you want. No one earns a place there through the use of force. Everyone must merit his or her place there and that merit comes only through love, peace sacrifice and service to humanity as well as tolerance while you are in that world down there. All that must come only from the heart and motivated by the freewill of the individual. Tell me something; what did you do to the 'infidels' who at the end of your deadline still refused to accept your religion?

Sandi: We either chopped off their fingers or hands or legs or gave them another deadline. If they never complied, we then killed them. That was called cleaning up our creator's kingdom in preparation for a pure faithful generation of servants.

Messenger: Something still bothers me about those people you had to force to accept your religion and those you had to kill because they refused your religion. Didn't they have a religion of their own?

Sandi: They had.

Messenger: Then why did you think that yours was more important or the only true one that led to our creator and not theirs?

Sandi: My Spiritual leader said that the only true religion was the one he belonged to and acted as its spiritual leader. He had a dream and it was to get everybody on the surface of the earth to belong to our religion either by peaceful means or through the use of force. Besides, there were those who did not have any religion and were pure pagans. What was wrong with bringing them into the light and giving them hope for salvation?

Messenger: There was nothing wrong with bringing people from darkness into light. There was something wrong in the way you went about it. As I said before, they had to move from darkness into light out of their freewill and not through the use of force because my master is interested only in what comes from the heart and done out of freewill. You had no right to impose your religion on others. (*Pauses for a while*) So, to get people join your religion, you instituted an atmosphere of fear by burning down houses of prayer which belonged to those you considered enemies or pagans. You used explosives in most of the destruction and many people were killed. Was all that really necessary? Must you use force in your desire to save somebody. Must you burn down the houses of prayer of those you considered pagans, infidels or enemies?

Sandi: My spiritual leader said that the only language some people understood better was the language of brutality. That was the fastest means to get people convert to my religion.

Messenger: I know there were men and women who were born in your religion and prayed the same way you did. But they still suffered the same fate you reserved for the so called 'Infidels' who did not accept your religion. Why was that? If at the end of the day, even those who belonged to your religion were not spared, who then was safe?

Sandi: We had to kill some of ours because they behaved badly. They housed or provided a hideout for the infidels we gave an ultimatum to. That was a crime our spiritual leader could not pardon because it was an act of betrayal. We had to carry out his wishes.

Messenger: What about the woman doctor and that primary school girl you personally cut their throats? What was their crime?

Sandi: That woman was too stubborn. She was ordered to stop practicing as a doctor and she refused. The job of a doctor was reserved only for men. By refusing to stop, she was indirectly telling us that she was equal to men. That was intolerable. Concerning the young girl, I had to kill her to serve as a lesson to others who disobey our orders. Girls are not supposed to go to school. They already had their task which was well spelt out by our spiritual leader. They are just to make babies, raise them, and take care of their husbands and their homes. Out of those, they were not supposed to aspire for anything else. Those women who go through school tend to argue with men and sometimes openly challenge men. What would have the world become, if there was conflict between women and men? It would have turned up side down. We saw the education of women and the girl child as a threat to world order and most importantly, a threat to our tradition and way of life. So, it was good to stop them when they were still very young.

Messenger: So, by killing them under the pretext of setting an example, do you really believe that you did the right thing?

Sandi: Of course since the Spiritual leader said so. After the executions, many women doctors like her either resigned or fled the country. Many young girls stopped going to school and order was restored. Nothing was under threat again. I think it was the right thing to do. Do you see things differently?

Messenger: Yes, I have a contrary view. When my master made man, He took a rib from the side of the man and it was very close to the heart which He used in making the woman. Taking a rib close to the heart had a lot of significance. It meant that the man had to love the woman. She was not supposed to become an object or slave who had only to be seen and not to be heard. The man has to love her and treat her with dignity. That woman you killed was just continuing my master's healing mission. She did nothing wrong and was a threat to nobody except your pride. Besides, education of the girl child has never been a threat to any man and any society. You and your spiritual leader created an imaginary threat and were afraid of it.

Sandi: It's a pity you see things that way.

Messenger: What happened to Penn Khan?

Sandi: He was a very nice boy, I must say. His father was rich and we needed money to keep the spread of our ideology going. We resorted to kidnapping and the parents of any victim had to pay a ransom we asked for against the promise of seeing their loved one again. Penn Khan was really an unfortunate case because we lived in the same neighbourhood and he knew me. If I released him after his parents paid the ransom, he would have revealed my identity and I did not want that to happen. I felt terrible killing a

11

twelve year old boy but I did not have many options to choose from. I had to do it. If you were in my shoes, you would have done the same thing.

Messenger: Really, you think? What was the last thing you did before coming here?

Sandi: The infidels were becoming too many. It seemed that when we killed one, fifty others joined them. Some joined them out of sympathy. The worse thing was that they even converted people from my own religion. They even afforded themselves the luxury of building their own houses of prayer. The court even passed a law granting them the right of worship and protection. The culture and ways of life of the infidels in different countries where they were in the majority was not helping matters. Their women danced and walked in the streets naked. They even put on clothes which were meant for men which was intolerable. They put such attires on the internet and people of my religion especially youths copied them. The culture of the infidels was too invasive. My spiritual leader saw it as a threat to our religion. He advised us the soldiers of our creator to take action both at home and abroad. He made it clear to us that we were at war and any of us who died on the battle field would go straight to the house of our Creator because we were fighting a just cause. The Creator would then crown us martyrs and give each of us many virgins. So, with those promises in mind, we went out for war. I strapped explosives round my waist and entered the house of prayer of the infidels and blew myself up. I'm sure none of the infidels went out of that house of prayer alive.

Messenger: (*Seemingly curious*) what did your religion preach?

Sandi: It preached love for the faith, its prophet, the creator and fellow brothers and sisters as well as tolerance.

Messenger: Don't you think that your actions went against those fundamental principles that your religion stood for?

Sandi: Not at all. All those who belonged to our religion were loved and tolerated. Those who did not belong to it were enemies and infidels. If they were infidels, they were enemies of our creator and had to be eliminated. We had to do the elimination in the name of our creator who spoke to our spiritual leader in a dream and gave him the command.

Messenger: Can I say something? To me, religion proclaims first love for the Creator and then love for fellow human beings and tolerance for what they are. Isn't that correct?

Sandi: That is a summary of what I have already told you but you have left out the fact that it has to be for people who practice the same religion.

Messenger: I have the impression that our conversation will have no end. Let's leave that one aside for a while. What happened to Thomason Jose?

Sandi: He was an infidel and wanted to get married to a woman who belongs to my religion. That was an abomination. It was not proper for holy people to be mixing with pagans and infidels. My spiritual leader vehemently condemned it and we made it known to Jose. He was given options to choose from. Option A was that if he wanted to marry the woman from my religion, he had to first of all convert to my religion. Option B was that if he did not want to convert, he had to give up his love for the woman and marry another woman who was a pagan or infidel as himself. He preferred option B but was not prepared to give up the woman who belonged to my religion. There were consequences and he knew them. We had to kill him to teach him a lesson and to deter others who had the intention of following his example.

Messenger: Two grown up people fall in love and decide to get married. You and your spiritual leader take it upon yourselves to decide whether they get married or not and you used religion as a separating tool. Who asked you to play such a role?

Sandi: I have the impression that you forget so soon. I've earlier told you that my master received instructions from our creator in a dream. He had to prepare people for our creator's kingdom to come by doing away with pagans and infidels. If he had to allow holy people to hook up with pagans or infidels, how was he preparing people for such a kingdom then?

Messenger: My master made man and woman and asked them to go and people the world. He was by that creating the institution of marriage and blessed it. If two people decide to marry, they should be allowed to do so because they are marrying for the glorification of my master and not for the

14

glorification of your spiritual leader and you. Don't you think that religion was supposed to be a uniting instead of a divisive factor especially in the institution of marriage?

Sandi: (*Remains silent staring at the messenger*)

Messenger: Instead of using religion to unite people, you used it to bring separation among them calling some holy people and others pagans and infidels. As far as the institution of marriage is concerned, religion, social status, race, origin and financial conditions are not supposed to be an issue. My master blesses any marriage so long as there is love, honesty, sincerity, dedication and respect of the rule laid down by my master and not your spiritual leader.

Sandi: You seem to be against all what my spiritual leader preached and stood for.

Messenger: I'm not the one who is against it but my master. Now tell me, do you think our creator was pleased with your actions?

Sandi: (*with a smile*) Of course and he is supposed to reward me by crowning me a martyr and surrounding me with many virgins for my pleasure. So, when are you taking me to Him? I'm itchy to get out of this place. It does not resemble one bit the one my spiritual leader talked about. He painted a picture of a golden city with our creator sitting on a throne with many servants around Him. I don't think the place is as hot as this one. Please take me there.

Messenger: Have you forgotten so soon? Remember I told you that once you get in here, you never get out again. Well, I'm sorry to inform you that there will be neither a crown nor virgins for you.

Sandi: (*smile dries up. looks very worried*) .Why do you say that? You are not the Creator, are you?

Messenger: I'm not the creator. I am His messenger. He sent me here to point out your mistakes if you feel that you have no reason to be in here. If He preferred that you come here, it is because He did not approve of your actions down there. He wanted everyman to do just ten things to make Him happy. His fifth command was that no man was allowed to take a life. By killing so many people and taking your own life, you went against that fifth command which made my master very unhappy. That is not all, by taking your own life; you deprived your son of a father and your wife of a husband. That child and wife were beautiful flowers in my master's garden and your job was to take care of them to grow. Instead of being a father and husband or the gardener, you abandoned it and were doing what you were not assigned to do. By breaking up marriages in the name of religion, you destroyed the foundation on which my master's holy family was to be built.

Sandi: Please wait, wait, wait! Are you trying to make me understand that I sacrificed myself for nothing?

Messenger: If you had died in the course of trying to save someone from armed robbers, a wild animal, a ruthless government system, a collapsing building, an oncoming

16

vehicle, that would have been a worthy and noble sacrifice. Your kind of sacrifice was motivated by pride, revenge and the glorification you would get from men. You do not turn houses of prayer into blood baths and you call it a sacrifice. My master was not anywhere in that picture.

Sandi: What are you telling me? Does it mean that my spiritual leader lied to me and many others?

Messenger: I'm afraid he did not only lie to you but he equally misled you.

Sandi: (*Unable to stand on his feet*) If my spiritual leader lied, he should be the one to be punished and not me, right? I was only following instructions.

Messenger: Well, that is the reason why my master endowed each and everyman with a brain. If you were mentally impaired, that would have been a different story. You had the choice either to use your head and spare the lives of your victims or not to use your head and follow blindly the instructions of your spiritual leader. You decided to follow his instructions to the latter. You called some of your comrades who took their own lives in a huge explosion alongside the lives of thousands of innocent people as martyrs. You sent congratulatory messages to encourage your other comrades who tried to kill thousands but were unfortunate to have been stopped. You called them heroes and used your tongue to motivate the young and gullible minds to join your ranks. That praise for carnage was very disheartening to my master. Converting people through the use of force was wrong. Using explosives to destroy the

17

prayer houses was wrong. In many parts of the world even right now, some of your comrades are still burning houses of prayer belonging to their brothers whom they consider as enemies. They kill thousands in the process. Let me tell you that all those still indulging in such horrible acts would atone for their actions when they leave that world. Landing here is the outcome of your actions while you were down there.

Sandi: So what is this place?

Messenger: It is called the Land Of Eternal Discomfort. If you will excuse me, there is someone who would be knocking on that gate soon.

Sandi: (*Stops the messenger as he tries to leave*) Please wait, I would want to give that spiritual leader the beatings of his life. You would direct him into this place when he comes, right?

Messenger: I am not the one to direct him here. Where he goes from there depends on him. If towards the end of his days down there he regrets his actions and begs sincerely for forgiveness, our Creator can forgive and take him in. Our creator is very merciful when you ask for forgiveness from the bottom of your heart. But you must do that down there and not here. If you had made good use of the brain our creator endowed you with, maybe you wouldn't have been here.

Sandi: (*surprise*) what!!! Our creator would take him in if he regrets his actions and begs for forgiveness sincerely? After all what he has done? I can't believe it.

18

Messenger: Oh yes… that is what it is. To you and your brothers down there, once someone has been brandished a criminal, he ceases to be human. He becomes a subhuman or worse still, reduced to an animal stripped of every dignity. He is discriminated upon in all aspects. My master looks at things from a different angle. When He gives sunshine, its rays touch everybody. When He gives rain, it falls on the roof of each and everyone without exception, whether good or bad. That is to tell you that my master's ways are not the ways of man. He does not want any of his sheep to be lost.

Sandi: (*Heart broken and full of regrets*) why was our Creator so dormant? I did all those things which I've now realized were terrible in his name and he just sat there watching. Why didn't he do something to stop me?

Messenger: It is not true that he just sat there watching. He did indeed try to stop you.

Sandi: How?

Messenger: Through your son who kept running after you and crying not to go out each time you had to go and carry out your spiritual leader's orders…. Through your wife who cried most nights complaining of your neglect…. Through your friends and relatives who tried in vain to advice and to talk you out of what you were doing…. And even through your late mother who came to you in your dreams pleading with you to be her once good son again by doing what was right. That is how my master tried to stop you.

19

Sandi: Can I have some water?

Messenger: You saw already that the tap isn't flowing and I don't know when it will. You just have to be patient.

Exit messenger

Sandi: (*jumps out of the hot room. Watches messenger as he walks towards the gate. Sees messenger go through the gate without opening it. Falls to the ground*).

Curtain

Act Two

Scene 2: This Scene Opens With The Messenger Leading The New Comer In.

Stone: Where are you taking me?

Messenger: I'm taking you to your room.

Stone: (*Looks at the surroundings. Sees the dusty floors, broken windows and doors and collapsing walls*) oooh no! This place is not good for me. Even a prisoner would not like this place. What's worse, the place is unnecessarily hot. I'm going back. (*Starts walking back towards the gate. Messenger does not try to stop him. Gets to the gate and tries to push it open. It doesn't open. Takes a few meters backward with the intention of using his body as a weapon to knock open the gate. First and second attempts fail. Gives up and walks back to where he left the messenger who is now in the company of Sandi*).

Stone: The gate didn't open.

Messenger: I noticed.

Stone: And you didn't come to help me open it?

Sandi: That gate only opens to let people in. Once in here, you can never get out again. That's what I was told when I got here.

Stone: (*Looks at the Messenger*)

Messenger: What he has said is right. Now can we go and see your room?

(With no other word, all three head to the room next to the one given to Sandi. Inside, there is a broken couch with the materials on it torn and old. There is an air conditioner which does not work and is covered by rust. The floor is dusty and untidy).

Stone: *(Not happy with what he is seeing).* Before I came here, I lived in a big mansion which was all covered with tiles. There were many servants to clean it. No grain of dust could be seen. If I saw any trace, the servant who was supposed to be in charge was immediately fired. The chairs in my sitting room were first class. *(With disgust)* look at what you have here….a single couch which is old and torn. *(To the Messenger)* Why did you direct me in here when you knew quite well that your furniture was not up to date?

Messenger: When you were born, you were born with nothing and in the course of your life, you amassed a lot but when you died, you took along nothing. You entered here with nothing and you should be contented that you even have a torn, old couch. You've done nothing to earn it. I think you should really count yourself lucky.

Stone: Did I hear you mention the word lucky? I don't think somebody should be talking about luck in this hole which is not good even for a rat. I have lived through life and had a taste of nice things. I know what is nice and what's not. This place is not nice. It sucks totally and completely.

Messenger: Well, the choice was yours. You were told when you were growing up that there were two places you go to when you die. The good place was called Land of Eternal

24

Happiness and the other one was called Land of Eternal Discomfort. You were seriously warned about the latter but where you go after you leave that place below your feet depends only on you.

Stone: I've just told you that I was living like a king down there and knew the taste of good things. I wouldn't have possibly chosen this place. It sucks. No man in his right senses would choose a place like this. If at all I chose this place, I must have certainly been drunk.

Messenger: That is not true. You were not drunk at all. You were in your right frame of mind when you decided to come here. All those who have come here keep claiming they never chose this place. Instead, they accuse me of directing them here. It's true that no man in his right senses would choose a place like this one but each and everyone is the driver of his or her own life.

Stone: (*To messenger*) What are you doing here? Did you decide as well to come here?

Messenger: I am a messenger. I was sent here to take care of some people who might be contesting their presence in this place.

Stone: He who sent you did the right thing. I am one of those who can't remember the day, time or year I decided to come to this filthy place. If you can refresh my memory, I would be really grateful.

Messenger: Well, let me begin with a phrase somebody you knew very well made. He said "All Men Are Born Equal." By implication it means that all human beings must be treated fairly without prejudice of any sort and with dignity."

Stone: I disagree with that. He who made that stupid statement was my one time leader. He did not really mean what he said because his actions proved the contrary of what he was trying to preach. He claimed all men were born equal but had men who were forcefully taken from their homelands working on his plantations without any pay.

Messenger: Whether he put into practice what he said or not or did the opposite of what he preached is not the issue here. I am using the phrase because it is very true and suits the purpose for which my master created Man. You consider the phrase stupid. What do you consider stupid about it?

Stone: Where he said that 'All men are born equal'. That is ridiculous… there are those who must be servants or slaves and others who must be masters. There are those who must be rich and others who must be poor. There are those who must think and make proposals and others who must execute the proposals of the thinkers. There are those that must be loved and others that must be hated. In such situations, you cannot talk of equality. Have you tried to imagine a world where everybody is materially or financially rich? Such a world would be chaotic.

Messenger: (*Smiles*) I like your explanations. But there is something you've said there which is really intriguing and it is that 'there are those that must be loved and those that must be hated'. Who are those that must be loved and those that must be hated?

Stone: I wouldn't like generalizations here. I will take myself as an example. When I was down there, I loved those that were like me, rich like me, civilized and belonged to my class. I hated those that were poor, different, uncivilized or inferior.

Messenger: Can I ask you a simple question?

Stone: Please go ahead.

Messenger: From the moment you were born till the moment you left that world, did you eat just one kind of meal day in day out?

Stone: Please come on!!! That question is ridiculous. We had a saying down there that 'Variety is the spice of life.' If I ate just one meal all my life, I would have died of constipation prematurely. Anybody who wants to live long must eat varieties.

Messenger: That is something which is well said. Well, my master who made you and me love variety too. That is why he made all those people that you hated because they were classless, poor, different, uncivilized and inferior. What bothers me right now is why you loved variety and my master's own love for variety had to be such a huge problem to you. By hating them, are you by implication trying to tell me that my master shouldn't have created them?

27

Stone: ooohh no!!! I think you are getting it all wrong. I am not against the fact that the odd category was created. On the contrary, it was a good thing people like them were created. For example they made us, the privilege group, feel important and also did the jobs we considered odd jobs.

Messenger: I'm glad you admit that they are important because they are useful.

Stone: There you are wrong again. They are useful but not important. People who look different, poor, uncivilized and uneducated are not important. You see, importance goes with class, respect, wealth, the kind of wife, house, car and kind of school one's children attend. If one is worshipped by the poor, the importance is even greater.

Messenger: wow!!! I am really marvelled. But, what I don't really understand is where that hatred for a fellow human being was coming from?

Stone: I hated some people who were different from me, who were poor and uneducated. They had a queer way of behaving. You needed to see what most of them did especially those that were uncivilized....they sacrificed some of their brothers and sisters in some stupid rituals and equally ate some of their brothers and sisters as food. Others strapped explosives round their waists and blew themselves up. Who in his or her right senses would do such things? How can one be talking about equality with such kinds of people? How can you expect me to associate myself with those low-lives? That is why we decided to catch them by force and use them on our large plantations as cheap labour.

28

Messenger: I've still not understood where that hatred was coming from. Was it just from the fact that they were inferior, uneducated or had some practices which you considered horrible?

Stone: At first I hated them because they were different, inferior, and so on. But it was that hatred that could give room to sympathy sometimes. What deepened my hatred especially for those that were different was the fact that our stupid representatives in the house of legislation decided to pass some stupid bills which they called the Bill of Rights. By the terms of the Bill, those low lives were granted equal rights as those of us who mattered in the society. The stupid things learned of it and wore it on their heads as caps. (*Really outrageous*) I couldn't stand it when my servants claimed rights when I asked them to do things they were already used to doing. They asked for payment for their services which they couldn't dare to before. The legislators went as far as fixing the amounts we had to pay them as wages. The worse thing was that a good number of those low lives and animals took advantage of the new laws to become influential, right to the extent that they became bosses and could dare look in the faces of their former masters. The one that really choked me was the right granting those animals citizenship. I couldn't believe that my nationality was given to those things we removed from one forest somewhere. That was all intolerable. I couldn't just take it lying down.

Messenger: That explains why you created an organization to sort of undo what the legislators put in place. Isn't that right?

Stone: I had to fight back. Those legislators thought they did what Napoleon left undone but they did not know that they were indirectly killing me with that madness they passed in the name of a Bill. Such an act inspired many other houses of Representatives around the world to do same. I started loosing millions in wealth and capital as labour became too expensive. Some of the fools who benefited from the Bill became rich like us and were helping many of their brothers to become rich as well. They produced what we produced and sold to their brothers. That was part of my market that was taken away. People like us were fast fading to the background as the trend continued. In different places where the same bill was passed, rich people there were wailing too. You can see that I was not the only one who suffered.

Messenger: If the cost of labour was too high and your wealth and capital suffered, why did you not try to negotiate with your former workers to give them a percentage of what they produced in place of the money you were forced to pay them as wages?

Stone: Do you know what you are asking me? Negotiating with them would have been begging. How do you want me to stoop so low as to negotiating with people I didn't even consider human beings? That was definitely unthinkable. I had to find another way out, by creating my organization with branches all over the world to combat the threat that was coming from those low-lives. I put in place the RLGO which stood for the Regain Lost Glory Organization. It had two branches. One branch was strictly military which had to execute our prescriptions and the other was the sensitization branch. I headed that second branch and developed the ideology of the organization. I trained followers who reasoned, acted and saw things the way I did. They had to go out to different parts of the world to spread my ideology. It had to do with the development of hatred for anybody that looked different and the separation of amenities. We could not use the same things with them. Those low lives were enemies and had to be treated as such. We could not succeed if someone who reasoned like us was not in a high place. So we imposed a compulsory contribution to our members and we used the funds collected to sponsor some members who became heads of state and members in the House of Representatives in some countries around the world. The military branch on its part was asked to kill some of the low-lives that had become prominent and also create an atmosphere of fear by burning down their homes and issuing death threats. That way they could not aspire to become prominent or dream of anything great. They had to be contented with what we produced and not to aspire to become producers. They had to remain eternal consumers.

Messenger: Did you consider yourself after doing all that a successful man?

Stone: That is a very good question. Yes, I succeeded to a greater extent. I had a large following both at home and in different countries around the world. Thanks to the actions of the military wing of my organization, some of those low-lives got back into their shells and as a direct result, I regained part of my lost market. Because they could not aspire for higher heights, the changing times forced some of them to come back to me for jobs and I trapped them with loans which they couldn't pay back. Anybody who couldn't pay his or her loan was forced to work on my estate until he or she could pay it. I presented the papers of the loans given to them to any government official who came around my estate to see if I was keeping anybody against his or her will. I bought some of government officials outright with money and convinced a good number of them to join my organization. My deficits were quickly covered and my business began booming again. My followers who became heads of state or members of the House of Representatives did a marvellous job. They voted into law my famous principle of separation. There was separate development and separation in the use of public facilities like hospitals and schools. It was abnormal that real people should be using the same facilities as those low lives. In addition, we could do whatever we wanted with those low-lives but if they spoke to us without permission or respect, they were immediately put to death. I think I succeeded largely on that front.

Messenger: Did you at any time try to fit yourself in the shoes of those you considered enemies?

Stone: Why was I supposed to do that? Those were people who wanted to put me out of business and you are asking me if I tried to feel for them? I couldn't feel for them. I could have feelings only for those who were like me in pain and agony because of the madness of our legislators.

Messenger: Did you believe that there was a creator who created you and I, including those people you call enemies?

Stone: Well....yes. I was told in the house of prayer I attended that there was a Supreme Being who created

32

everything. I don't know why he had to create those ones that were different, poor, uneducated and uncivilized.

Messenger: So, to you He shouldn't have created them?

Stone: It would have been better if He hadn't created them. Can't you see that they were pests and trouble makers?

Messenger: But you needed those 'enemies' as labourers on your estates as well as a market for your products, not leaving out the fact that you needed them to feel important. You ate the food that your cooks prepared with their hands. You benefited from their labour which you exploited. You benefited from the natural resources tapped out of the regions the low lives came from. You benefited from the trade between your country and theirs. I would have thought that since you hated them for one reason or the other, you would have kept them out of every picture. I mean… not sell your products to them, exploit their labour, and so on. What would have happened if the Supreme Being hadn't created them?

Stone: (*Scratches his head*) Well, if it was for the purpose of labour and market, He had the right to create them.

Messenger: I see…one last question: Did you love your creator?

Stone: What a question… I think it is the same as asking me if I loved my mother. The answer is a big YES. That was the first thing we were taught in school and houses of prayer. I loved my creator very much. He is the ultimate destination

Everyman wants to get to. But wait a minute….since I came in here you've been bombarding me with questions. Do you have a problem with the way I lived my life?

Messenger: Do you really want to have an answer to that question?

Stone: Yes.

Messenger: Alright… I will give you an answer. I would like you to sit down because I wouldn't want anything to distract you.

Stone: *(walks to the couch. Contemplates whether to sit on it or not. Finds the couch too dirty and decides to remain standing)*

Messenger: Half bread is better than none. You must learn to love that couch as it is.

Sandi: *(walks and sits on the couch)*.

Stone: *(looks at Sandi with a stern expression on his face)*.

Sandi: *(leaves the couch and remains standing)*.

Messenger: You would remember that somewhere in the course of our conversation, I told you that I could not understand why my master's love for variety had to become a huge problem to you in the course of your life down there. He created everything you saw including those that you called enemies with love. It was your place to treat all those people and things He created with dignity. My master is very please

34

when he sees that all what He created is treated with dignity. Instead, what did you do? You brandished some enemies simply because they looked different, were poor, were uneducated and had a civilization you considered primitive. Let me tell you that when He created you, He breath into you so that you would have life. He did the same thing with those people you considered enemies or low-lives. Breathing into you so that you could have life meant that He lived in you just as He lived and lives in every one of them. With such a behaviour I wonder how you can now claim to have loved my master whom you've never seen during your life time when you could not love some people you could see under the pretext that they looked different, poor, uneducated and primitive. Listen, my master measures your love for Him through the love you show to your brothers human beings. By rejecting those people, it was my master, our creator you rejected because he lived in them.

Secondly, when my master's servants came to you to tell you that all human being were created equal, you grew furious and had them kicked out. When your leaders and some members in the House of Representative passed Bills to make your treatment of the so called low-lives illegal, you referred to them as mad men. They simply wanted to reinforce the wishes of my master. You thought it unimaginable for someone to tell you that you were equal to those 'low lives.' And even right now, you are still arguing for the sake of argument. Well I will explain how equal all human beings are.

Stone: I am all ears

Messenger: You are made using the same material….soil of the earth. You are all born of a woman. You are all born

35

with nothing. After living for some time, you all die. After death, your bodies return to the earth where you were taken from. Your blood is red. You all have the ability to speak and reason. You do not choose your parents and do not decide the day you die. All these are what connect you human beings as equals. You refused to see them and focused only on what your eyes could see. You saw and defined them by their poverty, illiteracy and uncivilized nature. It's true that they looked different, they were poor, they couldn't read and write but that didn't in any way cancel the fact that you were all equal in the eyes of my master.

Stone: I don't see why you keep trying to defend what cannot be defended. Things are so clear for you and me to see that all human beings were not born equal.

Messenger: That is not true. Let me buttress my point with an example you knew so well. Your mother was a business woman who started trading in ice cream ever since you were a child. You grew up to know that ice cream was white because your mother made hers and used only the white colour. When you grew older, you picked up a girl friend called Tania with whom you decided to go on a trip. When you got to your destination, it was too hot and you decided to go for ice cream. When you got to where it was sold and requested to be served, you were given ice cream which had a different colour from the white you grew up knowing. The one which was given to you had a pink colour and you refused to touch it because it was not white. Your girl friend was served with one which had yet another colour. Hers was brownish. You called the young man who served you and asked him what he would call what he served you.

36

He told you that what he served you was called ice cream. But you still could not believe because you had it in your mind that anything ice cream must be white in colour. You even tried to stop Tania from eating hers but she was stubborn and urged you to taste yours. When you did, you realized that it was not different from the one your mother made though it had a different colour. Do you know why the name of those ones could not be changed from ice cream to something else? It was because the main ingredients remained the same. The colour was just a minor ingredient and it was not even the principal ingredient among the minor ingredients. That's why the taste remained the one you knew though the colours were different. You human beings are like that ice cream having main and minor ingredients which my master used in creating you. You left the main ingredients which united all of you together and concentrated on the minor ones which sort of disunited you. You had the opportunity to taste what was served to you in a different town and after tasting it, you saw that it was indeed ice cream. Did you give the opportunity to those people to prove their worth before brandishing them low-lives?

Stone: Your explanation on the ice cream is very true. But when you try to connect it to us humans, it does not fit. Do you know why? It is because your equality theory does not fit as well. Now tell me something… if our creator created us and wanted us to be equal, he would have made everybody rich. But He didn't. Why?

Messenger: Have you yourself tried to picture a world where everybody is materially rich? That is a question you've asked not long ago. There would be chaos and my master was aware of that and had to make opposites. You would realize that for example the poor were always where the rich were. You could not find a materially rich man without finding many materially poor people around him. You could not find an educated man without seeing many uneducated men around him. You could not find a civilized man without seeing many uncivilized men around him. You could not see a financially rich man without seeing many financially poor people around him. That was no coincidence. It was my master's design to test your generosity, selflessness and love. You were supposed to use what was given to you, to serve humanity. If you are a rich man and you hate somebody else because he is poor, then use some of your wealth to make him what you expected him to be. There is nothing wrong in doing that. That was what you failed to do and are still here contesting my 'equality theory' as you put it. You yourself just said a few minutes ago that some of those low-lives became prominent as a result of the madness of some of your leaders. If they could become prominent, it means they were endowed with the same creative and managerial abilities as you were. They too went to school and became pilots, doctors, engineers etc. What could you or your likes do that they couldn't? That still goes to show that you were made equal and endowed with a common ability......reasoning. Do you know why everybody could not be rich? It's because everybody could not be a doctor, or a business man or a teacher. If everybody were to become a doctor, who would be a teacher, engineer, or pilot?

Stone: (*Bends his head and stares at the dusty floor. Opens his mouth to speak but the words do not come out. Remains silent*)

38

Messenger: (*Continues*) So, my master did not create people and make them materially rich because He knew what creating people and making all of them materially or financially rich would engender. That's why he made some people different, poor, uncivilized and uneducated. It was out of my master's love for variety that things were made that way and I don't see how that was supposed to become a problem to you. (*Reflects for while, Smiles uneasily*) isn't it strange that you showed so much love towards animals but couldn't show some love towards your fellow brothers simply because they were poor or looked different or uneducated? You participated in voting laws protecting the rights of animals but you denied the same rights to your brothers because of some trivial reasons. You were given the right to do whatever you wanted with animals from creation including killing them for food. But you were forbidden to kill your fellow human and it was well spelt out in the fifth commandment. If you can kill an animal for food it means that it is not supposed to be more important than your brother for what ever reason. If you could give rights to animals, what more of your fellow brothers? Up till today, some of the sons and daughters of those you hated because they looked different do suffer all forms of discriminations especially in work places or job offers though they may have the same qualifications, talents or better. Only some jobs that are considered inferior are reserved for them. My master's heart bleeds when He sees all that. Hating your brother because he looks different, inferior, uneducated or uncivilized is telling your creator that you do not appreciate his own love for variety. In that case, any man who hates his brother for whatever reason has a case file to come and face here once he or she crosses that bar that separates this world from the one you just came from. That brings us to your third transgression.

Stone: (*Raises the head and stares at messenger but does not say anything*).

Messenger: Because you did not consider some of your brothers as human beings, you created an organization through which you tried to undo what my master came down there in person and established. You tried to do away with the one thing the world desperately needed and still needs…love. When my master created man, He gave to him ten commands which He wanted man to carry out so as to glorify Him. It seemed man could not understand the commands and had difficulties practicing them. So after a while, my master decided to come down there in person and during His stay there he decided to summarize His ten commands to just two. The two commands were all centred around one thing only….love. That is, love for Him our master and love for our fellow human being which he sowed in the hearts of men. You tried to uproot it through your ideology of hate and separation which you spread around the world. By doing that, do you know how many people you sent down the path of destruction? Did you ever sit back and think of its impact in human relationship? It almost destroyed what my master established. By planting the seed of love in the heart of Man, my master wanted him to see his fellow kind as a brother, sister, neighbour or friend. And what did you and your ideology do? Your preaching led to the history of lynching in America where killing somebody because he or she looked different became a favourite sport. It also led to the execution of over six million people from the same

40

household in Germany during the second world war, the mass deportation of Chechens in the former USSR out of pure hatred for them, massive killings in the Balkans especially Serbia, the Rwandan genocide, many terrorist attacks around the world etc. In some countries some people kill others for a reason as minute as 'he or she physically looks different.' That was not what my master wanted. What He wanted to see was love like the one among a football team made up of players from different nationalities when a goal is scored….the innocent love among children when they are playing. The irony of all what you did was to carry your gospel of hate and separation right inside houses of prayer where the walls of separation, class distinction, social status, race and ethnic differences had to be torn down. The house of prayer was supposed to be a sacred sanctuary where only those who recognized my master in everyone came for worship. The most aching of what you did was that you implanted your seeds of destruction even in the hearts of innocent children. It is a terrible thing to mislead children. It would have been better if you were never born.

Stone: (*Raises his head and looks at the messenger*) That last statement shows that you've condemned me already and I don't think you are in a position to do that. It is our master to come and condemn me.

Messenger: That was not the only disheartening thing you did. The government knew that you were a farmer out to curb hunger but what they didn't know was that you cultivated more than just crops. You farmed what was used to produce cocaine and marketed it all over the world. You knew the bad and addictive effects of such a drug. You knew that those who consumed that product did not do so for medical reasons but used it to escape from the difficulties of life. Yet you went ahead to make money out of it at the expense of human life. Those who tested it became addicted to it and used it to auto destroy themselves. Men, women, children.... That was no different from suicide and you assisted them by providing what was needed to take their lives. You who provide the destructive ingredients are as guilty as the one who uses them for self-destruction. Of course, you were not interested in the bad effects of cocaine but in the money you generated from it. You used it to fund your organization and gave the seeds to others in different countries. Today in many countries, people fight and kill each other over it. Combating the production and consumption of cocaine is proving really difficult. With the advent of technology, some of your followers catch people who look different, execute them, while at the same time, video tape their acts and then post them on the internet. When they leave that world, they would account for their acts. However, do you think my master would be happy with you for doing such things? Yet you want my master to come here? He does not come here. But if he were to come, he would ask you just one question. "What did you do with the children I sent to you?" What would you tell Him? Would you tell Him that you turned them into objects of hate and destruction? Is that what you want Him to come and hear? He will never come here. The fact that, that door opened and let you in is a clear indication that He did not approve of your actions. He created all human beings with the differences which lay only in what your eyes could see and gave them different personalities. You were supposed not to merely tolerate them

42

but love them and never let unity pass you by. That was what you were supposed to do. Did you do that?

Stone: (*remains silent*)

Messenger: Any man who follows your preaching and hates another man for whatever reason has a case file here in the world beyond to face. When my master came down there he asked everyman to love his neighbour as himself. That was a divine command and an open door for you to use in entering (*pointing*) that golden city over there. It was made on the basis that every human person intrinsically commands some respect no matter his or her size, age, race, or position of work or society. Take away that respect and you reduce the individual to a beast. So what you had to do was tear down the walls which might have been erected between you on the basis of colour, race, religion, sex, material and economic status. That is to say that the fact that you were an employer was not supposed to make your employee a lesser human being. In the same vein, a house owner should not consider his or her tenants as mere beggars; a houseman or wife should not consider her housemaid little less than a slave; a political, traditional, religious or public authority should not bring his or her subjects to the level of mere listeners who are never heard.

Exits the room leaving stone and Sandi

Scene 2: Still in Stone's room

Stone: (*To Sandi*) why are you staring at me like that?

Sandi: Because of all what that Messenger said to you. Are you convinced of all the transgressions he said you committed?

Stone: Why do you ask? Is it because I kept arguing? It is in my nature to argue even when I know that what is being said is true. Of course I am convinced. I did all those things he said but it's too late now to make amends.

Sandi: (*Extending the hand*) I'm called Sandi:

Stone: (*Takes the handshake*) and I'm Stone.

Sandi: Nice meeting you stone.

Stone: (*Furious*) Did I just hear you say nice? What is nice about this encounter? It seems you still do not know what you are in. You are in this hole meant for rats with no prospects of ever getting out and you are talking about nice?

Sandi: (*Startled*) Hei! Hei! Hei! Brother, I'm not responsible for your being here and don't see why you want to take it out on me.

Stone: (*Calms down*) Sorry about that. You know it's not easy to be living in affluence and within a twinkle of an eye you find yourself with nothing and being forced to answer tough questions. It really makes me nervous. Sorry about that.

Sandi: It's ok. Since you cannot have what you want here, like what you can find.

Stone: You know quite much about me concerning how I got here. What did you do that landed you here?

Sandi: I did some things which I've come to realize were really terrible.

Stone: What kind of terrible things are you talking about?

Sandi: I killed young girls who disobeyed my orders by going to school and women who were already professionals and refused to quit jobs I considered to be for men. I equally killed people who were not of my religion and members of my religion who collaborated with them.

Stone: What did you have against girl children going to school and educated women occupying posts of responsibility?

Sandi: My spiritual leader told me that girls who went to school opposed their husbands. They were supposed to be seen and not to be heard and education was changing all that. The women who held posts of responsibility became models for others who aspired to become like them. When we asked them to quit their jobs, it was intended to kill the aspirations of those who wanted to be like them. They were a threat to our authority as men and we couldn't just let that happen.

Stone: .... And those who did not belong to your religion?

Sandi: They were considered infidels who could not inherit the kingdom of our creator. We had to eliminate them so that only those who were considered worthy were allowed to live. That messenger told me that I had no right to do all those things.

Stone: I disagree with the fact that ALL what we did was wrong. At least we did some dignified things which have to be considered.

Sandi: If your problem is with the word 'All', it does not matter. But I think most of what we did was wrong. I think that messenger was right otherwise why are we here?

Stone: (*Remains silent for a while in a pensive mood*) I think we are brothers in crime.

Sandi: What do you mean by brothers in crime?

Stone: I mean we had a lot in common. We were afraid of anything that was different, we killed people, we wanted to maintain our supremacy and last but not the least, we were all afraid of change and used all the means at our disposal to combat it. But unfortunately change was the only thing that remained permanent. Now that we are speaking, all what we fought to preserve is fast being relegated in to the backyard of history.

(As they sit talking, they can see Messenger and another person pass outside heading to another room).

Sandi: I think we should go and see that guy who has just walked in.

Stone: That's a good idea. I think we can forget about thirst and hunger if we are constantly busy. Let's go

They both Exit.

Scene 3

Messenger: (*Introduces William to his room*)

William: (*Enters the room. There is nothing as furniture. The walls are perforated and the floor is very dusty. William goes in reluctantly and stands in the middle of the room peering around with a very disgusted look on his face*).

Messenger: That is where you will have to put up.

William: Please, is there no other room better than this one?

Messenger: I'm afraid not. You sent absolutely nothing here for us to prepare for your coming.

Enter Stone and Sandi while Messenger exits.

William: (*Looks very afraid and runs to one end of the room*) who are you guys and what do you want?

Stone: Don't be afraid. We are not going to hurt you. I'm called Stone (*pointing to Sandi*) and this is Sandi: We are your neighbours. We arrived here…. (*can't say when exactly*) since there is only continuous day light here, it's difficult to say when we came. But he came first and I came after him.

William: (*Feels less threatened and introduces himself*). My name is William. When I saw you guys walk in here, I thought you were coming to torture me.

Sandi: Well as you can see, we are not torturers. Did the Messenger tell you why you were sent in here? We all know that you are not happy to be in a place like this. No normal person would be.

William: I don't need him to tell me why I'm supposed to be here. I know why I'm here.

Sandi and **Stone**: (*Surprised…simultaneously*) you know why you are here? How?

William: In that world down there, I was master of the law. I knew what was morally right and morally wrong. I was charged with deciding the fate of people who were accused or suspected of committing crimes.

Stone: Are you telling us that you made the conscious decision to come to this place?

William: Not really. Sometimes you know the right thing to do but you fail to do it. Instead you do what you are not supposed to do. It is like wanting to succeed in an academic examination but failing to read. By failing to read in preparation for the exam, you've prepared to fail. We humans were made and punished with too many weaknesses. The major ones were those of the flesh and love for material things as well as love for power. Once you allowed those I've just enumerated to dominate you, you became disinterested in what was morally wrong so long as you stood to benefit from them.

50

Sandi: But I thought having the knowledge of what is right and wrong should help you avoid a place like this.

William: Yes I agree with you. But being armed with the knowledge of what is right and wrong is not enough. You would be gravely mistaken if you think that having the knowledge of what is wrong or right would make things easy for you. On the contrary... the more you become aware, the more it becomes difficult. Do you know why? It is because you would have to constantly battle with yourself. Battling means you would try to fight yourself not to seize that power, money and all the many other beautiful things life can offer which unfortunately were there in abundance and my job gave me the opening to grab more, more and more. The temptation was so great and I had to take advantage of it and live life to the fullest. I saw that fighting the temptations for the sake of honesty, honour and moral uprightness as useless and senseless. Anything that was morally acceptable depended on the whims and caprices of those with physical, economic, judicial and political might. I was one of them.

(*Sandi and stone are listening with mouths open. They are almost dreaming*)

Stone: So what did you do that brought you here?

William: I worked in the courts and had the responsibility to either free or condemn someone everyday that went by. That had to be done after all evidence had been laid down and proven beyond every reasonable doubt. But...

Sandi: (*Interrupts*) But what? You didn't look for evidence before condemning people?

Stone: (*To Sandi*) can you be quiet and let him speak? When you keep interrupting him, my thirst comes back and I don't want to think of it when the tap is not flowing.

William: (*Surprised and unhappy with what he just heard*) what did you just say? Did you say there is no water? I'm really thirsty too.

Stone: If you continue with the story on how you got here, you will not feel it. You were on the point of verifying evidence.

William: Ah yes. I was saying that the evidence presented in court whether true or false did not matter to me. All that mattered was the amount the plaintive had to pay for a case file to be opened and the fines the defendants had to pay when charged. The court premise was never a place where justice was served but a place where a lot of money was made. Nothing went for nothing. I set booby traps for anybody who came into the court premise either to complain or to defend his or herself.

Sandi: What sorts of booby traps did you set?

William: No one could wear shoes which made noise when he or she was walking in the court premise. Anyone who entered in any office and sat on a chair without permission was asked to pay a fine. Anybody who came in to complain or defend his or herself and spoke without being asked to do so had to pay a fine. No mobile phone could ring and if it happened even by mistake, there was a fine. I did nothing to publicize my self-made rules and regulations. They were out to fetch money for me. Any signature, pen or ink or piece of paper was paid for. All those who worked with me were very happy because they shared all they collected into three parts... one for me, one for the state coffers and the last one for themselves. The court was really a money making institution. I became addicted to money. The more I had it, the more I desired it and the more I reinforced my booby traps to obtain it. I weighed the pockets of any two individuals who came to me with a problem. The one who had more money won the case. There was no justice for the poor. My numerous booby traps scared many of them from the courts. I had no use for the little salary the government paid me.

Stone: What did you do with all the money you collected?

William: That is a timely question. That is where I was driving to. With all that money, I lived the best life any normal human being could really dream of. I travelled to any country I wanted to, at any time I wanted. I drove in the most expensive cars and built many mansions in my home town. The one I lived in was a come and see. It had a name which eventually became the name of my neighbourhood.

Stone: What about those who were already incarcerated and were awaiting trial? Did you use them to make money too?

William: I did not spare anyone. There were thousands who came to court over ten times but I kept adjoining their cases. I wanted them to pay a huge amount of money from which I could have a share. You know, the state had a huge percentage of the fines the courts charged criminals and I had to make mine behind what I charged. Those who were rich quickly got a trial and had their sentences reduced to base minimum. Some simply bought their freedom and got out of prison. For those that were poor, they had their cases adjoined several times. The intention was to get them to pressure their family members to bring money. That's why some of them could spend up to five to ten or more years in prison without trial. I turned the wives of some of the poor men in prison into mine and had children with them. Some beautiful women who ended up in prison but were poor became my concubines and I equally had children with them. From the last count before I left that world, my children numbered 60. I just couldn't keep my hands off the ladies. My job really gave me the power and opportunity and I seized it.

Stone: And your wife in all that?

William: I had many concubines outside but they could not replace my wife. She was meant for my home to take care of me and my legitimate children. She cried many days and nights because she wanted me only for herself but I had a contrary view. With money, power and wealth, I considered myself a gift to all women. She ended up developing high blood pressure as a result of my actions. She is still there battling with it. I think it will end up claiming her head.

Stone: From the way you sound, it seems you do not regret coming here.

William: Far from it. Nobody would live a life of affluence and all of a sudden descend into misery and be happy. My life down there was not the best and I was aware of it. It was a life of vanity because what I had as wealth was acquired through illegal means and the justice I applied was that of money. The power I had through my job as well as the money, made the women flock to me because of what I had and that made the temptation too great. I lacked self discipline and allowed worldly pleasures to condition my way of life and reasoning.

Stone: Were there no protests against the way you did things or managed the courts?

William: There were oppositions. There were protests almost on a daily basis against the amounts one had to pay to lay a complaint or defend oneself or have a document signed. Of course the police were always called in, to disperse the crowds. Those that tried to offer stiff resistance were arrested and I decided their fate. With demonstrations not working, the people resorted to writing petitions. Many of them were sent to the government to have me removed but nothing of that sort happened. Do you know why? It was because the government badly needed me. Those in power wanted to remain there for as long as forever and needed me to help shut up some of those who were eyeing their posts.

Stone: How did you do it?

William: It was quite simple. The government wanted to remain in power by all cost and so became very uncomfortable with the educated class. As a result teachers, lecturers, journalists, philosophers and opposition leaders became targets. Any of them who openly criticized their way of doing things had to either be bought over or killed or locked up in prison for as long as possible. Any aspirant who could not be bought over was sent to me with strict instructions concerning the verdict. I then had to charge him or her with any crime and decide the number of years he or she had to spend behind bars after fabricating evidences or buying witnesses. Very recalcitrant ones were sent to their graves directly and indeed they were in their thousands. For those who I really wanted to make them feel that I had their lives in my hands, I put them on death row and did not tell them when they would be executed. Some of them had to stay for years and I knew the impact on their psychology. It is terrible going to sleep without knowing if that would be your last night alive. That anxiety and uncertainty kills faster than any poison.

Sandi: If you knew that putting them on death row and not informing them of when they would be executed was too torturing, then why did you do it?

William: I don't know….may be I enjoyed it. To make matters worse, I informed some of them of their executions only one or two hours before it was carried out. I loved when they were like butterflies in my palm and I could do with them whatever I pleased. I was a product of a system that killed people. Such a system was inhumane and it helped to shape me.

Sandi: I think my methods were better because I did not subject my victims to that kind of torture. I used explosives which killed most of them instantly or a knife to cut their throats and they died shortly after.

Stone: Were there any formal trials for critics of the government and potential aspirants?

William: Only when there were too many eyes on us especially those of the international community and campaigners for the respect of human rights. Most of the trials were done behind closed doors. In most cases, there were no trials. We simply produced documents which the accused merely had to sign with no questions asked. We presented such documents to the international community as proof that the accused actually acknowledged their faults.

Sandi: listening to you, I have the impression that I did not do anything.

Stone: Really... you think? I think what you did was worse.

William: (*To stone*) What did he do?

Stone: From what I gathered, he allowed a crazy fellow he called Spiritual leader to mislead him into killing innocent girls and women for just being females.

William: Kill girls and women for being females? Did they want a world just for men or what?

Stone: They did not want girls and women to go to school and their reason was that women were going to challenge their authority as men. Those that disobeyed were brutally killed. Besides, they killed other people in the name of religion. If you belonged to another religion, you were automatically an enemy and had to be eliminated. His spiritual leader claimed our creator instructed him to do so and my friend here was one of his greatest agents.

Sandi: (*Looking annoyed*) you are talking about what I did with a lot of pleasure forgetting about the terrible things you also did.

Stone: You provoked me to do so by comparing what you shouldn't. By telling him what you did does not mean that I'm any better. What I also did was terrible.

William: (*To Stone*) What did you do that brought you to this place?

(*Stone does not reply immediately and all three remain silent for a while*)

Stone: Well, I was a wealthy man too before coming here. I was a farmer who did agriculture on an industrial scale. I forced people to work for me because I did not consider them human beings. I hated them because they were given rights, they looked different, they were uneducated and uncivilized. I personally ordered the deaths of thousands and indirectly caused the deaths of millions around the world through the ideology of separation and hate. I came to learn here that we were all equal and I had to use my wealth to make those I hated what I wanted them to be. (*To Sandi*) That messenger forgot to say that I made so many people that really looked different from me hate themselves. I made them believe that if they were not like me, they were not human beings. That pushed millions of them to delve into cosmetic pane-biting which of course had very devastating effects. I created an army to spread my gospel of hate to all nations which resulted in the killing of millions worldwide. (*Remains in a pensive mood for while*) that was not all, I erected very high fences between me and those I hated so that even their children could not come into my territory to beg. For those that forced their way into my house because of hunger, I had them locked up and fortified my fences with armed guards, wild dogs and barbed wires. At the same time, I used them as my market and exploited their labour. I really frustrated people. . But that one was mild. I was interested in expanding my business and that necessitated more land. So, I seized the lands of the poor communities that settled around my large estates. Those that resisted, I looked for their source of water and contaminated it. That forced them to go and I took over their lands. After claiming the lands, I cut down every tree to make way for the planting of cash crops that would give me a lot of money. There were cries and campaigns against deforestation but that did not mean anything to me. I was a farmer and business man and anything that stood on my way had to be cleared by all means available.

William: That was really cruel, I must say. Goose pimples would cover anyone's body who listens to all what you did.

Stone: There you are. When you listen to what I did, you forget what you did.

William: Sorry about that.

Stone: (*face brightens up*) Do you know what that Messenger would have told you if he were here to hear your story?

William: No, can you tell me?

Stone: (*Tries to imitate the Messenger*) you are here because you did what you were not supposed to do. You were supposed to defend the poor against the rich, the weak against the powerful, the common man against the government and the exploited against the exploiters. Instead you joined the exploiters to exploit those who could not fight for themselves. You were supposed to use your office to serve and not to be served. You were supposed to use your office to make friends especially with the underprivileged but you used it to make enemies and instead to serve, you wanted to make the people feel how important you were. All your life, you served a well to do minority group against a vast majority you were supposed to serve.

Voice of the Messenger: You have spoken well.

(*All three run to one end of the room quivering with fear. They can't see him but can still hear his voice*).

Voice of Messenger: Do not be afraid. I am not going to hurt you.

Sandi: (*To William and Stone*) do you think we can trust that guy?

60

William: You can see that we really have no choice. We are completely deprived of rights here. We had rights down there and refused the same rights to others. Since we could not feel what those people we subjected to pain felt, we have to feel it now. That guy is the only one we can communicate with now. We have to trust him whether we like it or not. If he has said he is not going to hurt us, we have to take him for his word. So chill guys.

Stone: Before I forget, there is one question which is still troubling my mind. I am here because I was obstinate and blind to see other people as my equals. I was also very obsessed with class and social distinction which made me internally blind. There you can see that there was an umbrella of ignorance which covered my vision. My friend here was misled by someone he put all his trust in blindly. He too was suffering from chronic ignorance. But this was not the case with you. You knew what you were doing and knew very well that it was wrong. Before you came here, didn't you try to implore the mercy of our creator?

William: I must tell you that I had the visit of so many men who claimed to be servants of our creator. They belonged to many religions but they served me with conflicting messages. The first one that came to me told me that our creator could only forgive transgressions which were committed out of ignorance. Since all the transgressions I committed and still continued to commit long after he left were not committed out of ignorance, I considered myself doomed forever. Many others came after the first one and told me different stories. Some said that there were some transgressions which could not be pardoned by our creator. I committed some of the transgressions they cited as examples. Yet there were others who came and told me that there were no transgressions that our creator couldn't forgive but that He could forgive only after certain conditions were met like my begging for forgiveness from the men in prison whose wives I slept. That was something I could not do no matter what. I was worried about my reputation. The last thing that finally confused me was science that tried to prove that everything we had down there resulted from evolution. That science theory suited my conscience and it made me less guilty since I did not know who or what to believe. The words of the first servant of our creator who came to me kept echoing in my mind and I knew that I was already condemned. I did try to go to the house of prayer. I knew at least how to pray but failed several times because my restless conscience wouldn't let me be. As a result, I was gripped most of the time by the syndrome of procrastination. I was finally banished from below there by prostate cancer and I left without begging for forgiveness. (*Sighs*)

Sandi: I understand your frustration. I came with high hopes of being crowned a martyr as well as to be given so many virgins for my pleasure.

Stone: Where? Here?

Sandi: Yes of course.

(*William and Stone explode with laughter to the extent that Stone rolls on the ground. Sandi looks very surprised as he does not see what is funny in what he has said*).

62

Sandi: What is it? Have you guys started losing your heads?

William: (*Still laughing*) where did you get that idea from? How can it even cross your mind in a place like this?

Stone: (*To William*) Maybe we should try to grant one of his wishes by giving him a crown.

William: I think you are right. (*Runs out of the room and finds some dry grass which he uses to make a grass crown. Brings it to the room and place it on Sandi's head. They all bow to him as a king*)

Stone: It's a pity we can't find virgins around here. But I think half bread is better than none. If you can't have the virgins, well, you have at least the crown. (*Bows again*)

Sandi: (*With a disgustful look on his face*) I dreamt of a golden crown and with the virgins fanning me and bathing me. Not this shit you guys are doing here. You are just mocking me. (*Sighs*) I think I should go to my room and try to get some sleep.

(*Just as he is about to exit, they hear the crackling sound made by the gate*).

William: I think someone is to be let in.

Sandi: let's go and see who it is.

(*They all exit William's room*).

Act Three

Scene 1: At the Gate.

Messenger: This way please.

Carlos: I can recognize that gate. It looks like the one leading into my palace. But I can see only a vast yard with no tiles and the nature of the structures leaves much to be desired. They are not good for human habitation especially for somebody of my rank. Where have you moved my palace to?

Messenger: Nobody has moved your palace. It is still where you built it.

Carlos: Then where is it?

Messenger: It is in the world below your feet.

Carlos: Then what am I doing here? I don't remember asking anybody to take me anywhere. Someone must have kidnapped me from my palace. (*Stops and thinks hard for a while*) But how is that possible? I have the best trained guards in the world and kidnapping wouldn't have been possible. (*Thinks and rethinks*) How did I get here?

Messenger: Nobody kidnapped you. From the way you sound, it seems you don't even remember what happened to you.

Carlos: It seems I don't know what happened to me? (*Remains silent for a while. Searches his brain again and again*) Aaah

67

yes, I was addressing a crowd at the capital city square when a flying object was spotted heading towards me. The last thing I can remember was a huge loud? noise the flying object made upon touching the ground. Could it be...

Messenger: The flying object was a missile and it catapulted you here, not instantly though. You have moved from that world down there to this one.

Carlos: But I didn't ask to be sent here. Those who used that missile to catapult me here did so without my consent. I want to go back to my beautiful palace. That is the only place where I feel really comfortable and safe.

Messenger: alright, see you soon.

Carlos: (*walks back towards to the gate. Murmurs to himself as he does so*) My goodness, what a place!!! Even the house of my dog is better than this place. And he is trying to say that we have two worlds we have to live in. If this is the one someone has to leave and come to, then it is of no use. It is better someone remains down there. It seems the president of this place is not a serious man. He has not built a palace worth the name even for himself because I can't see any good structure anywhere. This place looks like a slum. If I have to accept that nonsense of moving to this next world, what would my people think of me now? I brutally shut up those who tried to say that there was a supreme being some where greater than me. I couldn't tolerate that and had many of them killed. I am the only supreme one who is the giver and taker of life. My people all know that and I have to keep it that way. This is not possible! If this is the palace of that Supreme Being those foolish religious fanatics talked about, then I think he needs to come to me for some lessons about living in a luxurious house. This place is not good for human habitation. (*Gets to the gate. Tries to open it but it doesn't open. Tries to use force but it still does not open. Shouts to the messenger*) Come and help me open this gate. That is an order.

Messenger: (*Does not move but remains rooted where he is, just watching*)

Carlos: Is this real or I'm just dreaming? Did that guy just disobey me? Down there, nobody could do that without having a knife go through his or her throat or a bullet through the head. (*Starts walking back to meet the Messenger*) Could it be that power is deserting me? I hate to feel that I'm not in control. (*Gets closer to the messenger and stares him straight in the eyes and says loudly*) Didn't I order you to come and open that gate?

Messenger: (*Remains silent and does not show any reaction*)

(*Stone, Sandi and William come closer to where Carlos and the Messenger are*)

Carlos: If this guy does not want to go and open that gate, you three should go and do it. That's an order? (*They do not move and remain staring at him. They start laughing at him*) is this stupidity or outright stubbornness? If Combo was here, all of you would have been dead by now. I would have asked him to take all of you to the guillotine and have your heads cut off for insubordination.

Stone: It seems you don't yet know where you are.

William: You are in the land of Eternal Discomfort.

Sandi: And once you get in here through that gate, you can never get out again.

William: We had a saying down there that when you are in a position of power, be wise and leave it before it leaves you. Power has forgotten you and the earlier you get use to it, the better for you.

Carlos: (*Not believing his ears. To Messenger*) Who are you guys... a relay team of the kidnappers? Where are you going to take me next?

Messenger: Nobody kidnapped you and you are not moving from this place. In other words, you shall never leave this place.

Carlos: What do you mean? What happened to my beautiful palace?

Messenger: What I mean is, the money, beautiful palaces, cars, politics, power and all the nice things of life belong to that world below your feet. You were born with none of them and you take none of them along the day you die.

Carlos: Are there no such nice things here?

70

Messenger: Well, there are. Those here are better than what you knew down there but they are not found in this part. (*Pointing to the golden City*) They are found over there.

Carlos: Can I go there?

Messenger: No you can't. You must earn your ticket into that place. You must earn it while you are down there in that world below your feet where your beautiful palace is.

Carlos (*Unable to continue standing on his feet. sits on the ground buried in his thoughts. The others retire to their rooms because of the intense heat leaving Carlos outside in the open yard*).

... ...

Scene 2 (still in the yard a long while later)

Messenger: Can I go and show you to your room now?

Carlos: Are you serious that once someone gets in here he cannot get out again?

Messenger: That is the way it is. That gate can only open to let people in but cannot let them out.

Carlos: Come on... certainly there must be a way. (*looks around to make sure that no one else is there to hear what he has to say. Almost in whisper*) if you open the gate and let me out, I will reward you greatly. I will send you any amount of money you want once I get back to my palace. All you need to do is to say the amount and I will send it.

Messenger: Money has no use here. It has great use only down there. You are prepared to give me any amount I want now. Is it your money you want to go and get to send to me? Of course not... it is the money of the poor tax payers which you have stashed in foreign banks. Those poor people contributed that money so that you would use it to build them hospitals, provide them with energy and good drinking water as well as roads. But you didn't. Instead you preferred to gather all the money and bank in foreign countries. All you were interested in was amassing money and more money. What kind of money did you really want? Money from the oil refinery went into your private account... you had a salary which was ten times that of your colleagues who governed countries richer and more developed than yours....your

73

presidency was allocated a huge budget by your rubber stamp parliament.... You had some advantages on top of all that.... And that was not all... you insisted on being the one to control the state budget which was again put at your disposal. Now you want to go and get part and send to me. But no...thanks... money has no use here and there is nothing you can offer me which my master can't. Do you want to go and see your room or not?

Carlos: Ok, I will follow you.

Scene 3: In the room Carlos is to occupy (The room is not very different from Sandi's with no furniture and only a bare floor. There is no window and the door is half broken)

Messenger: This will be your room for now. Do you have any questions?

Carlos: Can I have a couch on which I can lay my head?

Messenger: I'm afraid that is not possible. What you have been given is what you deserve. That is it. (*Exits while Sandi, William and Stone enter the room*)

Carlos: Listen boys, down there I was a president and I have billions kept in banks around the world. With that money, someone can buy a whole country. What do you guys say about getting rich and owning the best things money could possibly buy? If you help me to get out of this place I will give you any amount of money you want. I saw that crying outside there without trying to get out first was stupid.

(*All three explode with laughter. William rolls on the ground and continues laughing*)

Carlos: What is wrong with you guys? What is funny in what I've said?

William: I was master of the law when I was down there. I had all the money in the world. I could do whatever I wanted. But there comes a time when you must leave all those things down there. All those things belong to that world down there. They have no use here. Also, once you leave that world, you can never go back just as, when you enter that gate, you never get out. This is where you belong now. So try to get use to it.

(Re-enters Messenger)

Carlos: I thought you went to wait for others who might be coming in here at the gate. What are you doing here?

Messenger: (*Very calmly*) I'm here to clear any doubts that you may have in case you start feeling that you are here unjustly.

Carlos: There I think you are right… I'm here unjustly. I asked you to open that gate so that I could go back to a palace which cost me billions to build and you refused. In it, I have the same furniture that was made in the days of Louis XIV and my bed alone is the world's best. It is now empty while I'm here crawling on a bare floor which is very dusty.

Messenger: Who tells you that it is still empty? The person who has been fighting for decades to save the people from you now occupies it. The people really love him and see him as a saviour. He has started doing what you couldn't do for the people by respecting their wishes.

Carlos: (*Weeps*) how can that bastard occupy my palace? He does not even know how much I spent on it.

Messenger: It is not his place to know. He equally paid taxes which you used in building it. Anyway that is not what is important now. Tell me, why did you steal the poor tax payer's money and transfer it into foreign banks?

Carlos: (*Tears dry up*) I don't like that word steal. Don't you have any sense of diplomacy? That word is too degrading and only people who are suffering from chronic diplomatic illiteracy use it the way it is, especially with important people like me. Please, I did not steal the money as you put it. I took some which was at my disposal. I cannot steal what is at my disposal. As for why I had to put it in foreign banks, you know that politics is a very uncertain game. You can never tell which wind would blow you off at any given time. If a criminal like the one you say now occupies my palace were to come after you and you succeed in running out of the country only to find yourself in a strange one without money, tell me what would happen to you.

Messenger: Is that why you had to keep it in so many accounts in many different countries?

Carlos: Yes of course. When you are running for your dear life, do you choose where to run to?

Messenger: Why didn't you invest that money in the country you governed whereas you claimed to be its number one citizen? Why didn't you build hospitals, open up roads, generate power, create state owned corporations in which youths could find jobs or open schools where they could go in and acquire skills to become self employed? Don't you think that would have been a better way of spending that money rather than going to donate it to countries that were already rich? I'm asking because if you were doing the right things, no one would want to threaten you and you wouldn't be feeling insecure.

Carlos: How can you say that I donated my money to those rich countries? I merely gave them to keep and to give it back to me in due time.

Messenger: I've used the word 'donated' because you shall never go back there to collect it. If they do not feel sorry for your people and feel that there is no moral ground to send back the money, it will remain with them. They are not compelled to send the money back to your people. Anyway that is not the issue now. Do you know the consequences of stealing that money and hiding in foreign banks and not investing in the well being of your people?

Carlos: (*Bends his head looking at the ground and says nothing*)

Messenger: I will tell you. Thousands of young girls especially those that left school were not given the opportunity to be employed and so, turned to prostitution with some as young as 12. Their male counterparts became armed robbers and many others were forced to date women old enough to be their mothers. Many people died in hospitals because they were ill equipped and lacked even essential drugs. Thousands of women died on their way to the hospital to give birth because of the very bad nature of roads. Those that struggled and made it to the hospital ended up dying in labour rooms because those in charge were ill qualified. Why? Because they were the children of your brothers, sisters, friends and relatives who had to get into the training schools though my master did not destine them for those functions. Thousands died in their attempts to find a better life elsewhere through deserts. Many drowned in their attempt to escape the poverty you created for them by stealing their money and hiding in foreign banks. Thousands still take their lives even at this moment because they have lost hope in the future. You pushed millions to live in crime.

Carlos: I've told you that I did not steal but took. Your sermon is very touching. (*Pointing to Sandi*) I think if you continue like that he will soon start crying. From the way you are talking, anybody can understand that you know nothing about politics. You sound as if you wanted me or my government to employ everybody. That is not possible. In fact it is impossible even in those countries you referred to as 'richer than mine'.

Messenger: Is it because you couldn't employ everybody that you had to steal the tax payer's money and go and store in foreign banks? I know that it is impossible for any government to employ everybody. But all I'm saying is that you would have created or opened schools where your youths go and acquire skills with which they could survive on their own. With such skills they could either create jobs for themselves or move to an area or another country where their skills were needed. If you used or managed the tax payer's money only in educating your children of school going age and they acquired skills even if you couldn't employ them, nobody would have reproached you of anything. That would have been better than pushing them to foreign lands without the intellectual or technical know-how.

Carlos: I don't like the way you are sounding. You sound as though I didn't do anything at all for my people. I opened a hospital in every major town and city in my country...

Messenger: Which were ill equipped and the staff was not qualified. Do you know why they were not qualified? It was because they were mostly the children of your friends, relatives and party members. Do you know why being the children of your friends, relatives and party members made them unqualified? It was because while in the medical professional school, their parents prescribed the marks they wanted to see on the score sheets of their children. So the children knew that whether they worked or not, studied or not, their futures were guaranteed. You were aware of it. If you want to contest what I've just said, tell me how many times you went to any of those hospitals only for consultation when you were sick.

Carlos: Well, I admit that I had never gone to any of them for treatment or consultation. But I did not open them for myself.

Messenger: You really sound like a politician. You went to hospitals abroad which were well equipped and those who treated you there were very welcoming and very dedicated. You liked the way you were treated out in another country. Yet, you denied that same opportunity to your people. You did not want to offend your relatives, friends and party members by being hard on their children who worked in the hospitals. So, you let them do what they liked. Consequently, the hospitals were turned into money-making institutions and poor patients who could not afford the high consultation fees were assisted to their graves. That is what happens when people find themselves in places or posts they are not supposed to be in... they do the wrong things.

Carlos: But I opened one in the capital of my country where I built my magnificent palace and equipped it with the type of instruments I saw abroad. I got well trained workers and staffed the hospital with them. It served my people.

Messenger: You have left out so many things. You've forgotten to say that the hospital you are referring to was your private hospital which you didn't even go to for consultation. It served mostly your ministers and their families, friends, relatives, party members and big business men. The poor could not come close to it. In addition, you have forgotten to say that the well trained staff you talked about were not paid by the huge amounts the hospital generated but by the poor tax payer's money. Have I said anything which is out of place?

Carlos: (*Does not say anything*)

Messenger: The next thing you will say is that you opened professional schools to train youths who were to serve in different sectors of the economy. Well yes, you did open the schools but they were filled only by the children of those in high places.

Carlos: What was wrong with the schools I opened? Was it that I opened them or that they were occupied by the children of those I loved?

81

Messenger: There was no reason why competitive entrance exams into the professional schools you opened were organized and only the children of those in high places always made it. Those who scored very high marks had to be sidelined because they were children of poor parents or their parents belonged to the opposition or they did not belong to this or that social class. You knew there were irregularities through the protests and demonstrations that went on. You did something about it and it was to unleash the army on the protesters. That was not the right thing to do. You have to create a level-plain field for everybody. That was what you were supposed to do.

Carlos: (*Mockingly*) And if I did that, it would have cleared all the problems you have just enumerated, I suppose?

Messenger: I did not say that all the problems would have been solved. But they would have been greatly reduced.

Carlos: You are not different from that fool who called himself an opposition leader. He never saw anything good in what I did or in my government. He criticized everything and turned a good number of the people against me. Most of them started following him and did only what he said. I felt I was loosing control and had to take drastic measures. You are doing exactly the same thing. You disobeyed me and they (*pointing to Sandi, William and stone*) have followed your example. I have no authority here. If my military chiefs were here, you would have suffered the fate of that opposition fool. (*Stone, William and Sandi burst into laughter*)

Messenger: I believe that opposition leader you are referring to was Khan Hill. Tell us what happened to him.

Carlos: (*Mockingly*) you seem to know everything. Don't you know that one?

Messenger: If I ask you to tell me something yourself, it is not that I don't know but I want to point out your mistakes from what you say. You are given the chance here to say something but you didn't give that same chance to your victims. You decided what their crime was and the punishment that was meted out to them. They had no say. Can you tell us what happened to Khan?

Carlos: That fool had the guts to eye my throne...my birth right. He wanted to replace me by inciting the population against me. I asked everybody to dream and aspire to any post except that one. It was mine alone but he disobeyed me.

Messenger: Your country was not a monarchy but a republic. As a republic, there were rules which all republics came together and laid down. One of them was the organization of elections after a determined number of years. That means that the post of head of state had to be open to contest. If you wanted to be a ruler for life, why didn't you change the republic into a monarchy? That way, you could have claimed your birth right unopposed.

Carlos: I couldn't do that. The reason was that times were changing too fast and if I wanted to be a monarch, I wouldn't have had absolute power. The term 'Constitutional monarchy' became too fashionable everywhere around the world. Turning my republic into a monarchy and not dancing to the same rhythm would have been out of place. It would have attracted criticisms and that was what I hated most. Besides, if I turned my country into a monarchy, I wouldn't have been the one in public in front of cameras and making the major decisions. All constitutional monarchies gave that job to a prime minister who became the sole actor while the monarch was locked up in a palace feeling bored. That was not the life I wanted. I wanted to be in charge and to be noticed.

Messenger: Then maintaining the country as a republic meant you had to open the post of president to competition. You ratified the conventions which were laid down to that effect.

Carlos: In politics and international relations, accepting to do something is one thing and actually doing it is quite another. I was good at ratifying the conventions but my post was not to be opened to competition. I created a parliament which was there to do what I told them. Any motion which was tabled by individuals or opposition leaders had to be rejected especially if the motion was going to disfavour me in anyway. I put it in place because I didn't want to be brandished a dictator. I made all the decisions and the parliament was just there to endorse them.

Messenger: You were good at ratifying conventions and making promises which you hardly honoured. One of such conventions was the protection of refugees, mentally impaired people and underprivileged people. You left the refugees at the mercy of your uniform officers who exploited them in anyway they wanted. Whenever you had to receive a very important personality from abroad, you asked your uniform men to arrest all the mentally impaired people, beggars as well as all the young girls and women who were forced to sell their bodies for money in order to survive and lock them up somewhere. You considered them as dirt, dirtying the streets. Those were the people you were supposed to get closer to. Those were the people your way of doing things rendered in that state. You never asked yourself what role you played in their plight. You did not see them as human beings but rejected objects of the earth through which you could assert your importance. Tell me, how did you want people to know that you were that way and at the same time want them to continue entrusting their destinies into your hands?

Carlos: I never asked anybody to entrust his or her destiny into my hands.

Messenger: Any aspirant to the highest office does just that. Anyway, that is not the issue now. You still have not told us what happened to Khan.

Carlos: He violated a fundamental law by having his eyes on my birth right throne. By doing that he had to face the full weight of the law and I had to make sure that it was well applied. He was arrested and handed to the judges who found him guilty of treason which carried a death penalty. Justice was done.

Messenger: Did I just hear you mention the word justice? When you were down there, how much did you know about justice? Did you really mean justice or injustice? You saw Khan as an enemy. You asked your men to arrest him. You called your judges and instructed them to hand down nothing less than capital punishment. They took charge of organizing and acting out a piece of drama in the name of a trial, which was even behind closed doors. Those who tried him never knew him. They neither knew the neighbourhood he grew up in nor came from. Those who tried him were total strangers. Is that what you call justice? There were some actors too there and the name you called them was 'members of the jury'. When they could not be unanimous on a decision, they opened it to a vote as if somebody's life is something they can gamble with. Is that what you call justice? What was justice was what favoured you. Once anything was not in your favour, it was injustice. The courts were never there to render justice in the real sense of the term but to help you put away those you saw as enemies. The courts existed just as a window dressing for the international community.

Carlos: I thought there was some knowledge in your head. How do you expect me to be the head of the Judiciary and then the courts pass a judgment which disfavours me? How did you expect the judges whom I personally appointed to disfavour me? I appointed them to serve me. I had the right to fire any of them at any time when I had the impression that they were not doing their job.

Messenger: Let's leave out Khan, what happened to Wang Mills?

Carlos: That was the biggest fool who ever lived. He was an important committee member of my party and had many followers who were of his tribe. His tribesmen numbered over a million and that was an important figure to me when it was elections time though elections were just a formality. I made him minister and he used his position to open many businesses of his own. As a good tool, I exempted him from all taxes and gave him exclusive rights to supply certain goods. His people loved me just for the simple fact that I made one of theirs minister though they were not benefiting much from him. That made Mills think that he was indispensable and he grew horns. He dared to challenge me when I asked him to resign from his post of minister so that I could bring in someone else. The intention was not to offend his tribesmen who might have hated me for firing their son. He was too greedy and did not want to do it. I asked one of my servants to prepare a resignation letter on his behalf and he was forced to sign. The reason for his resignation was read on national television. As punishment for challenging me, I decided to have the amount of money he had to pay as taxes for the number of years he was exempted calculated. He was given a deadline to pay. He couldn't and I decided to seize all his businesses. In one of his business premises, there was resistance. There was exchange of fire between my men and his guards which resulted in the death of three of my men. He had no right to kill and I decreed that anybody who killed had to die.

Messenger: Did you investigate to find out if Mills was the one who killed your men?

Carlos: It was not necessary. If his guards opened fire, he certainly gave the order. Even if he didn't, give the order, the deaths occurred on his property and he had to pay for it?. Besides he had a lot of money which was enough to sponsor a rebellion against me. I had to keep him away by all means.

Messenger: Let's say he actually killed your three men and by law he had to face the death penalty. "Anybody who killed another had to die" that is what you've said. But you killed thousands. Why didn't you hand in yourself for execution because that was equally a violation of the law?

Carlos: Are you crazy? How do you want me to set a trap only to turn around and fall in it? Do you sometimes reason before asking your questions? I ordered people to be executed. I didn't go out cutting people's heads or putting bullets in their heads myself. So, I can still say that I didn't do anything and be logically correct.

Messenger: Mills supposedly killed three people and had to face the death penalty. You and your likes, who killed thousands remained free or in cases where you were toppled, you were sent on exile with huge material and financial benefits. Even your ministers who were accused of committing atrocities got promoted instead. That was the culture of impunity you promoted and it helped to push millions into the alms of poverty. Your men in uniform took advantage of it and committed all sorts of atrocities like summary executions, armed robbery, rape and extortions from those they were supposed to protect. When there were outcries against the impunity, you created commissions of enquiry. Those commissions rarely handed in any reports.

Even when they were handed in, they remained in drawers. The commissions of enquiry were just there with their long cutlasses to cut long stories short. Those that were killed or were victims of extortion were people that did not matter or were those in the opposition. Their woes benefited you and you would still call it justice if I ask you. But that kind of justice where the net catches only the small fishes and lets the big ones go through remains down there. Here, the story is different. Now, tell me something… did the killing of Mills bring your three men back to life?

Carlos: Not at all. I had to have him killed so that he couldn't be a threat to me and to others.

Messenger: Was he really a threat in the true sense of the word? Yet he had to face the death penalty. If you ordered the death of thousands only to end up entering the grave yourself, where was the sense or benefit in killing in the first place?

Carlos: The benefit was that those I killed did not disturb me or anyone else anymore.

Messenger: There you are right…a dead man does not disturb anybody. What happened to Goodwill Johnson?

Carlos: Ahh! That one too was a case. He was making a turn on the road with his car when my convoy was approaching. I was obliged to slow down because of that. I had so many enemies and they would have seized the opportunity where he was turning his car to kill me. I had to get out of my car and have him punished. He was supposed to bow as soon as he saw me. But he did not and that was crime number two. I asked my men to give him ten lashes of the cane after which I asked him to bow as the law specified. He still refused and told me that I was not his Master and he could only bow to his Master who was far greater than I was. He even added that his Master was omnipotent and omniscient and I was not qualified even to be His shoe cleaner. That was too insulting because I was the giver and taker of life and no one could possibly have been greater than me. I was head of everything like army, administration, judiciary, associations....in short everything. I spent billions making all sorts of portraits of myself and every home in my country was obliged to have one. My portrait was in every office whether private or public. No minister dared to say anything in public without mentioning my name. That way, my omnipotence was felt and my status of the giver and taker of life could not be challenged. I had to send him to go and meet the one he claimed was greater than me. What insubordination!

Messenger: There were some three hundred people who ran away from a neighbouring country into yours because they were being persecuted because of their minority status and religion. What happened to them?

Carlos: My eastern powerful and rich neighbour communicated to me that the three hundred people you are referring to were criminals. They were a minority group quite alright but they tried to fight for their rights the wrong way. They instigated violence which resulted in the death of hundreds. They got involved in unholy acts of suicide bombing and planting of explosives which killed many.

Messenger: Did you try to find out if what your neighbour said was true or why they had to resort to such 'unholy acts' as you call it?

Carlos: I did not need to know because I was not at the scene of the action. If my rich neighbour said that they were criminals, I had to accept it as the whole truth. After all, there were criminals everywhere. They were using the wrong methods to make their voices heard. Do you think I should have tried to know?

Messenger: That is the first thing any normal person would do. They resorted to violence because their land were invaded and seized, their women and girls were raped, and they were discriminated against in almost all spheres of society because of their minority status and their religion. When they petitioned the government, nothing was done. Instead, those of them who took the steps to petition the government were arrested and jailed without trial. That happened on several occasions and that was what opened the road to violence. When someone is pushed to the wall that is what happens….he fights back with all the methods and weapons at his disposal.

Carlos: Fighting against a government using violence was the worse thing they could do. There is no government that would tolerate uprising of that form or any other form. My neighbour told me that those that ran to my country for protection were criminals and that if I had them sent back to face justice, I would benefit from investments and financial aid. That was a very generous offer and I would have been insane to turn it down. So, I sent them back to go and answer for their crimes in exchange for what my rich neighbour promised.

Messenger: So, for investment and financial aid, you decided to sell people who ran to you because they were under the threat of being wiped out.

Carlos: International relation is a game of interest. There are gains to made and losses to be incurred. Either way, there is always a price to pay.

Messenger: That was a very bad way of looking at things and sending them back was definitely the wrong thing to do. Your neighbour was reputed for extrajudicial killings and you knew that sending them back was sending them to their graves. How were you sure that those you sent back were part of the unholy acts you talked about? The reason you advanced for sending them back when faced with criticisms was that they entered your country illegally. Trading lives for money is the most disheartening thing any man can do. You considered them criminals simply because your neighbour called them so. You could have at least given them the protection they came for and if you did not want to offer them the protection, you could have sent them to another country where the justice system was more humane. I will be back for us to continue this conversation. There is someone who is on his way here. See you soon.

(*Exit Messenger*)

Scene 4: Still in Carlos' room

Carlos: (*Tries to rally the others against the messenger*) Look boys, that guy is just bluffing. He can't do anything to anybody here. I had my popular slogan when I was still in my beautiful palace and it was that 'Unity is Strength'. I think if we unite, we will form a strong force. I think we can take that messenger guy down.

Sandi: How can we take him down?

Carlos: (*In a very low tone*) As soon as he walks back in here, the three of you can hold him down and I will land some serious punches and kicks on his head which would send him to the grave.

(*Sandi, William and stone burst out laughing*) what is funny in what I've said? Have I said something stupid?

Stone: (*Still laughing*) Oh no! Just go ahead and let's hear your plan.

Carlos: I've discovered that that guy is the one keeping us here. He is a wizard with very weak powers which we can overcome if we take him down. If we do that, we would be free to go and open that gate and regain our freedoms.

William: Can I ask one question? (*To Carlos*) That guy as you call him is alone against millions of us in this land and you think he is the one keeping all of us in here against our will?

Carlos: What do you mean by millions of us? I see only four of us here.

William: We are just close to the gate but there are more people as one goes inland. The heat is even unbearable as one goes further inland from here. These rooms are like offices where queries are taken care of before you are asked to go inland.

Stone: I also have a question. (*To Carlos*) If you say that guy is bluffing, weak and can't do anything, why do you answer his questions then?

Carlos: I answer his questions because I want you my boys to see that I did nothing wrong. (*With a smile*) What do you guys think of my plan?

William: I think that idea is a very stupid one.

Carlos: (*Very furious and tries to attack William but is stopped by Stone*) If my army chief was here, you would have been dead by now.

William: (*To Stone and Sandi*) Do you guys see? (*Pointing at Carlos*) He is just trying to use us in getting out. (*To Carlos*) I've just asked you if one man can hold millions of others against their will and you haven't provided an answer. Instead, what you want to know is what we think of your stupid plan. It seems you don't want to come to terms with reality. Everybody who is here except that messenger has died once and will never die again. This second world is divided into two sections... the right section and the left section.

94

Down there the preachers in houses of prayer made allusion to them and told us that anyone we chose to go to after death depended on the kind of life we lived down there. If you lived a life crowned with material wealth and you associated to it love for the creator and your fellow brothers especially the poor, generosity and selflessness in all you do, then you were going to find yourself in that *(pointing)* other part. But if you were blessed with material goods and you forgot about your creator, despised your fellow brothers because they were poor or different or for whatever reason, then this is where you will come. Yes indeed, all of us who are here did some terrible things down there... things that we were not supposed to do. Stop blaming that messenger. He is no wizard. Stop plotting to have him killed. It will never happen. He knows you are planning to do things and if you are not careful, he will step in here and tell you what you have been planning. Instead of wasting time thinking of something which shall never materialize, you should be thinking of how you will cope in here.

Carlos: Please stop trying to give me lessons. If you knew all that, how come you are here and not in that nice place over there?

William: Well, I am here because I did things I was not suppose to do and I have admitted that. But you continue to deny yours even when all the evidence is against you. What is wrong with you?

(Just then they see the messenger passing outside with the new comer following him) As I was saying, nothing can happen to you or anybody else here. You will feel hungry but there will be no food to eat but hunger will not kill you. You will feel thirsty

95

but there will be no water to drink but thirst will not kill you. You will feel like sleeping but you won't be able to sleep because of the intense heat. You will try to kill yourself but death will not come. That is what you should be preparing your mind to face instead of plotting some stupid things which shall never materialize.

Carlos: (*Gripped by fear*) are you saying that I shall never go back to my beautiful palace again?

William: I'm afraid you shall never go back. Listen, it was destined for man to live and die once. You have died and are now across the border between this world and that one below your feet.

(*Re-enter Messenger with a long sword in his hand.*)

Messenger: (*Hands it to Carlos*) You have been planning to kill me or should I say take me down?

Carlos: (*Lets the sword fall from his hand and it disappears as soon as it touches the ground. Falls to the ground*)

Messenger: (*To Carlos*) All your life, most of the things you did were those you were not supposed to. You killed people for various reasons which you were not supposed to. If you can remember, I asked you a while ago if killing Mills for supposedly killing three of your men brought them back to life and you said no. That means that the killing of the three men was wrong and killing Mills because he supposedly killed the three men was equally wrong. "Two wrongs cannot make a right" that is a famous saying down there which is

96

very true. Only my Master has the right to take a life since He is the only one who gives it. By claiming to be the giver and taker of life, you equated yourself to my Master which was a terrible offense. My Master gave life to each and everyone to fulfil a purpose. By killing anyone, you put your agenda ahead of my Master's own and as a result leave my Master's mission unaccomplished.

Carlos: (*trembling*) Are you saying that a man who killed another man was not supposed to face any punishment?

Messenger: Punishment, yes but death penalty, no. When my Master came down there and was about to leave, He appointed a successor. He told that successor that what he would bind down there on earth would automatically be bound up in the skies. The strings of successors have always been against taking a life for whatever reason and that is binding here beyond. It was not your place to take a life or to order the taking of one. Only my Master has the right to do so.

Carlos: What if the murderer escapes?

Messenger: A murderer can run away from fellow men but not from my master. He has a way of taking care of them.

Stone: What about imprisonment?

Messenger: Imprisonment is an option if and only if it is not used to put away those you feel are opponents. It is an option if and only it is not regarded as punishment. It is an option only if it is regarded as a reformation process in a reformation centre. That is, if someone steals because he is hungry and is caught and taken to prison, he should be trained to do something or acquire a skill which would enable him to be self employed once he gets out of that prison. Arming him with that skill will prevent him from committing the crime which brought him to prison in the first place. When you take someone to prison and after a while that person regains his freedom, you need to take the prison out of him. So, arming him with a skill is another way of taking the prison out of the prisoner. In the same way, if a man kills another man out of anger, make him to realize that what he has done is wrong and while in prison, train him how to control that anger. That way the prison would not be a place of humiliation but a place where human dignity is restored. But what happens down there is so disheartening to my master. Once someone has been brandished a criminal, he is automatically stripped of all his human rights. He is subjected to all sorts of inhumane treatment which makes my master very sad. Once someone has been brandished a criminal, it does not mean that all is lost as man sees it. That criminal is still important to my master. My master can still use what man has rejected to accomplish his mission.

William: Even murderers?

Messenger: Even murderers. My master's ways are not Man's ways. (*To Carlos*) You killed people because they were your opponents, they did not fulfil your political convictions or refuse to worship you. You forced many to lives their lives following your convictions forgetting those of my master. That was improper. That was not all; you refused to accept that there was someone greater than you were. Well, that person does exist and He is my master.

Carlos: So Goodwill was right? And who is your master?

Messenger: He is the one who created everything you see from the birds in the sky down to the fishes in the sea. He created everything including you who wanted to take His place and refused to recognize his existence. When you heard that He was omnipotent and omniscient, you multiplied your portraits and forced them on your citizens and made yourself head of all the institutions to make them feel that you were all powerful as well as the giver and taker of life. Anybody who did not abide by your rules was fired or sent to the guillotine. That was not all, apart from killing, dismissing and threatening, you equally had thousands of your opponents injected with poisonous drugs which engendered memory loss and forced them into mental institutions. When there were criticisms from abroad, you talked of destabilization plans to push you out of office. You banned all public demonstrations because you saw only the hand of destabilization. When you over looted the state coffers and criticisms followed, you still talked of attempts to destabilize your government. To you, all that was a game of politics and now you can see that the outcome is different. Since you lived your life in the belief that my master does not exist and have now realized that He does exist, it means you've lost everything. Here, you will have nothing.

Carlos: (*Desperate*) is there no way your master or can I say our creator, have mercy on me?

Messenger: I'm afraid it is not possible now. If you were still in that world below your feet, it would have been possible. But once across that bar, it is no longer possible. You got to power and instead of serving my master's people, you were busy serving yourself. You allowed power to blind you to the realities which laid bare in front of your eyes. The plight of the masses did not bother you. You used their poverty as a means to make them worship you. That power, it was my master who gave it to you to serve His people but you used it to make them feel how important you were. You even claimed to be equal or greater than my master who created you.

Carlos: (*exasperated*) please, please, please stop. Say no more. The words are piercing like a dagger through my chest. Why did our creator not stop me when I was doing all those terrible things?

Messenger: I have heard that question before and it keeps coming up. Let me tell you a little story…. There was a man called Ogun Wise who lived in the Northern part of the most populated country in Africa. I am referring to Nigeria. He was an old man but at the same time very wise. He was a moving library and went around the village and neighbouring villages answering all sorts of tough questions. That earned him the name 'Mr. Wiseman'. The villagers admired him and were proud to associate themselves with him. Each time he made his appearance anywhere, there were shouts to announce his arrival and all attention was tilted towards him. Not everybody liked him though… there were some whom out of envy hated him and did all they could to discredit him. One of those was Alamo Suleiman and he was bent on disgracing Mr. Wiseman in public by asking a question which he would not be able answer. So, one day there was a gathering as usual and all those present had exhausted all their questions and just when there was a lot of noise centred on the wise-ness of the old man, Alamo surged forward with his left palm closed. "Mr. Wiseman," he called out. "Here in my palm is a butterfly and I want you to tell me if it is still alive or dead. He intended to discredit Mr. Wiseman. If Mr. Wiseman said that the butterfly was still alive he would use his little finger to press hard on the head of the butterfly so that it would die. But if he said it was dead, he would just open his palm and it would fly off. Mr. Wiseman stood there speechless and the crowd became very quiet. Alamo asked his question again with an air of triumph. The old man took a deep breath and remained silent for a while. The crowd was watching. Then he opened his mouth and said "Well, whether that butterfly lives or dies depends on you because it is in your hands." That was not the answer Alamo was expecting and it kind of put him in a fix. He did not know whether to kill the butterfly or to open his palm so that it could fly off. He just stood there not knowing what to do. But all what I've narrated boils down to one thing…..choice. Alamo had the choice to either bury his envy and tap into the mountain of knowledge the old man carried around or to uphold his envy and find ways of disgracing the old man. In the same way, he had the choice to kill the butterfly or to let it fly off alive. You too had a choice and though your actions were terribly painful to my master, He did not give up on you. He still did all He could to stop you.

Carlos: How?

Messenger: Through the criticisms of those human right organizations, through the likes of Goodwill Johnson, through the journalist you considered as your worst enemies and those opposition leaders whom you killed and imprisoned. Strangely enough, you brandished those that opposed you as terrorists and enemies of the state. Those that succeeded to run away from you and died in exile were again declared as national heroes by you. You called them nation builders and fighters for change and justice whereas, in their life time, you called them enemies. All those who helped to track down your enemies and eliminated them were awarded medals and referred to as nationalists. Those who doctored election results and proclaimed you winner all the times were called patriots. When some of them died, you organized lavished state funerals in their honour with the tax payer's money whereas the tax payer wallowed in abject poverty. What would you call all that? Politics? Do you think my master was going to be pleased with such a way of doing things?

Carlos: Why did He not strike me dead or incapacitate me with a serious illness. It would have stopped me from doing such things?

Messenger: My Master would never do a thing like that. If He did that, He would have been interfering with your free will. You knew what was right and wrong but you let your love for money and power blind your sense of service to humanity. You did all what you did out of your free will. You had the choice to either treat your people the way you did or to treat them with all their human dignity in tact. You preferred to treat them like sub-humans. Some of your ministers went as far as owning brothels where young girls who were jobless were turned into sex slaves. They were chained to beds and rich foreigners who came into your country for business or international conferences were given the rights to do whatever they pleased with the young girls after they had paid huge sums of money. The young girls never saw the money which was paid because it was transferred straight into the accounts of your ministers. The worse thing was that some of the young girls used were as young as 12. You were aware of it and even slept with some of them too. Each time you left your palace and had to spend the night in some other part, town or village of your country, your men went to primary or secondary schools and sometimes universities and pulled out the most beautiful ones for you to spend the nights with. Those girls who were used as sex objects belonged to the vulnerable group. You were supposed to be a father and protector to them and punish all those who abused or tried to abuse them. Instead, you went …. (*Carlos Interrupts*)

Carlos: Please, can I say something?

Messenger: I know what you want to say. You want to say that you didn't know what you were doing was wrong. You and I know that is not true. You knew what you were doing. If you didn't know, why did you get your rubber-stamp House of Representatives to vote a law which stated that you could not be prosecuted for any crimes committed while you were in office? Why did you get them to vote a law which gave you immunity from prosecution? It was because you knew that most of what you were doing to your people was not correct and you were afraid that in the case where you were one day ousted, you would be asked to render an account. Well, here, the story is different. There is no immunity here. You answer for all the crimes your immunity protected you from once you get here. Everyman must render account.

Carlos: Is there absolutely nothing that can be done for me?

Messenger: Before you interrupted me, I was about to say that you had a friend in a neighbouring country who wanted to become president using unorthodox means and you accepted to help him. You saw it as an opportunity to get a share in the mineral wealth of that country. Your friend accepted to give you 30% of what you wanted if you helped him. You were never tired of amassing money and helped in toppling a government which my master's people chose to lead them. You sponsored a civil war in which billions were spent and thousands of people were killed while three-quarters of your own people lived in abject poverty. There again, you had a choice to either protect the interest of thousands by refusing to assist your friend take power through the use of force or to ignore the interest of thousands to serve the interest of one man. You preferred to serve the interest of one man. What happened to the displaced, women, children and the old men did not matter to you. You also had the choice to use the tax payer's money to reduce the high rate of infant mortality or reduce the high rate of mothers dying at child birth. But you preferred to use the money in buying arms to use in maintaining yourself in power. You had the choice to use the tax payer's money to improve the reputation of your country for having the lowest life expectancy in the whole world. But you preferred to use the money for enjoying yourself in luxurious hotels in foreign countries. Did you ask if there is anything that can be done for you? Well, kings, presidents and rulers of that world below your feet are known to live in all sorts of luxuries, enjoying all pomp and wealth. They are known to have taken everything for themselves, leaving their people in misery and poverty. They live in costly palaces surrounded by guards and servants. They block roads for their poor citizens for hours before and after their arrivals at ceremonies. The country or state is more or less considered as their private property. My master is greater than any of them. Yet he shouldered the burden of His subjects and paid the ultimate price to save them. Did you shoulder the burden of your people?

Carlos: (*Remains silent*)

Messenger: That silence speaks for itself. You burdened them with heavy taxes and used the money they contributed to enjoy yourself and make them feel how powerful and important you were. Well, landing here is the ultimate price and to answer your question, presently, I'm afraid there is nothing that can be done for you. As you can now see, my master created you without your consent but he can't save you without your consent.

(*Exit Messenger alongside William, Stone and Sandi*)

Carlos: (*Breaks down completely and sobs bitterly*)

Act Four

Scene 1: As the scene opens Vladimir is sitting in his own room and everyone except Carlos makes their entrance into his room.

Vladimir: (*To Stone*) I'm sure (*Pointing to the Messenger*) that guy is your servant but I found his behaviour very strange. He said nothing and remained quiet as a grave as he came to get me from the gate. He only acts. All through my life I have met people with different behaviours and I took them the way they were. I think I will have to tolerate him too. By the way, my name is Vladimir.

Stone: My name is stone and (*pointing*) this is Sandi and William. That one you have referred to is really a servant but not my servant.

Vladimir: He is a servant and whether he is your servant or not is not very important. Tell me, what is this place? Is it an inn or a resting place where people come and rest before continuing on their journey?

Stone: It is called the Land of Eternal Discomfort.

Vladimir: (*Smiles*) it's true that I've heard a good number of strange names in my life but that one is of another level. Couldn't you find a name better than that one to call this place?

William: Well, sometimes names are not just names but they actually tie with reality. How do you find the place?

Vladimir: The place is very hot and does not look at all like a resting place. But it is at least better than many places I lived and spent nights in, in my career as a man in uniform. Thanks to the nature of my job, I could survive anywhere. But for the intense heat, this place is not at all bad to me.

William: Well, good for you. You must really be the lucky one. I'm sure you were told down there that there were some two places people go to when they leave that world down there. Even if you never went to any house of prayer, you certainly heard from people in the street or at the barracks where you worked.

Vladimir: Yes I frequented the prayer house a lot. I went on week days and on weekends. I was told that there were two places, one for those who spent their lives doing what was good and dedicated themselves to the service of humanity while the other was meant for those who did all sorts of things that were not morally acceptable. The name that was given to the place good people go to was 'Land of Eternal Happiness' while the one for those who did terrible things was called Hell. No man in his right senses would prefer a place like that. I was told that nothing there goes the right way and the place is terribly hot. On the other hand, I was told that the place where good people go is bright and shiny like gold. Yes, (*pointing*) like that one over there. (*With an astonished look*) But then the distance to that place looks so short and I don't understand why we have to make a stop over here.

William: Well, as you can see, this is neither an inn nor a sort of resting place. I'm sure you were also told down there that where you go after leaving that world depended on how you spent your life down there. In other words, you had to use the life down there to prepare for the one thereafter.

Messenger: (*Pointing*) Are you sure the life you led down there made you worthy for that kingdom over there?

Vladimir: I'm sure... but wait a minute... why are you asking me that kind of a question? You are just a messenger... what do you know about living a worthy life or not?

Stone: (*Referring to the Messenger*) He knows more than you could possibly think or imagine. He is a Servant but not an ordinary servant. (*Pointing*) He works for the King of that kingdom over there where you are so desperate to get to.

William: If you say that you are worthy of that kingdom, that gate into this place wouldn't have opened to let you in. The fact that it opened and let you in is a clear indication that you are in the right place, which was dictated by the kind of life you led down there.

Vladimir: So what is this place?

William: This section where we are now is where all queries are taken care of. That is, if you feel you are in this place unjustly. After any clarifications, you will be asked to go inland.

Vladimir: (*Gripped by panic*) And if after verification, you realize that someone does not deserve to be here, would you open the gate and let him or her out?

Messenger: My master never makes mistakes. But if you have any doubts, we are going to examine your life down there together. Let' see, do you feel deep within you that you did your job properly?

Vladimir: I think so because that must be the reason why I rose to the rank of a colonel.

Messenger: Well, that was the appreciation of your superiors. What about the ordinary people? Did they appreciate you?

Vladimir: To be honest, not very much.

Messenger: That shows that there was a problem. The common people who appreciated you were just a handful. Do you know why things were that way? It was because you loved easy work and always sought the easy way out of situations. That is to say that whenever a crime was committed and the perpetrators left the scene without leaving anything which you could use to get to them, you became worried of your dignity. You were always afraid to be called incompetent by the population. So you devised a means to always get out. If the victim of the crime suspected anyone, you did everything to see that he or she was pinned down whether he or she was guilty or not. Investigating to see whether the victim of the crime's suspicions had any grounds was not very important. Where the victim of the crime could not think of any suspects, you found one yourself by planting incriminating evidence on any victim you picked with the help of your friends and you used physical torture to force him or her admit their guilt. When that was done, you always invited TV cameras and paraded the 'criminals'. That was how the authorities remarked you and you gained eventual promotions. Do you know how many innocent people you sent to prison and who are still there?

Vladimir: I might have been doing all that but I abandoned that practice after a while. You know that perfection is not human and if only a handful of people appreciated me, it was because no one man can please everybody. Besides, many people had problems with the law that I represented.

Messenger: My master does not expect perfection from any human. He is aware of everyman's short comings. But on the other hand, He wants everyman to put in his or her best in any work that is at the service of humanity. Did you put in your best?

Vladimir: We-e-e-e-l-l-l-l-l, I think I did.

Messenger: You are accepting with less conviction which means that you yourself are not sure. Let's see, what happened between you and John McLean?

Vladimir: He was my neighbour and I had a dream house I wanted to build for myself. My piece of land was small and I asked him to sell his to me and obtain another one else where. But he refused saying that he wasn't going to do it even if I paid him the world's money. I-I –I ….

Messenger: Finding yourself in a position of strength, you seized the land. Since your own land was small, why didn't you sell it to go and buy one elsewhere much bigger? Do you know what became of your neighbour as a result of your action?

Vladimir: (*Remains silent*)

Messenger: Well, he was forced to go back to his village where he sunk into frustration and finally died of stress. You took away the only hope he had for his wife and children. Let's leave your neighbour aside…. What about George Kim?

Vladimir: A lady mistakenly accused him of unlawfully taking her radio set. I picked him up and locked him in my cell. After some investigation, it was established that George had an identical set and that the lady's radio set was actually taken by her younger brother.

Messenger: Did you release George as soon as you realized that he was innocent?

Vladimir: (*Remains silent*)

Messenger: You didn't. You waited until an amount which you called 'bail' was paid. You forced him to pay it even though you knew he was innocent.

114

Vladimir: But that was the system and I was not the only one doing it.

Messenger: It was the system and you knew that it was wrong. But because you benefited from it, you kept it alive. Many people died in your custody because you always said that they were worse than rats. You considered them outcasts simply because they were brandished criminals. You did not allow those that were sick to take their medicines and the money and food which their relatives brought for them became yours. That was not all....you equally siphoned gifts and funds given by humanitarian groups for the upkeep of the prisoners. All that could be called greed but to me, it was man's inhumanity to man. I don't know what you would call it. That too aside, what about Sergio?

Vladimir: He was an illegal immigrant. He had no valid documents and by law, he had to be behind bars.

Messenger: But that was not the reason why you locked him up. You locked him up because you wanted him to surrender or part with any money he had on him. Unfortunately for you and him, there was no money and you left him in that cell for three days and three nights with no food or water. He had to sleep on bare floor.

Vladimir: You sound like you wanted me to take money out of my pocket to provide him with legal documents or food. That was not my job.

Messenger: I didn't say that you had to provide him with legal documents using money from your pocket. But what would have been wrong with you doing so? You knew very well that he was vulnerable without documents and you decided to take advantage of it. That is where you went wrong. Did you even bother to find out why he left his country to find himself in yours without documents? Yet, you locked him up for three days without food or water. He slept on a bare floor. That was inhumane treatment. The fact that he never had documents didn't mean that he ceased to be human. Besides, why do you think he fell into your hands and not the hands of another?

Vladimir: I think it was just coincidental and he was unlucky to have been caught.

Messenger: There was nothing coincidental about it. It was my master's design and he wanted to test your humanity. But then, you did what you were not supposed to do. You were supposed to fight for those who could not fight for themselves, protect those who could not protect themselves, help those who could not help themselves and seek justice for those who were persecuted. That was a divine ordination. That's why you were strong and powerful while those who came to you and some of those you confronted were weak. You and I know that I have cited just three cases but there were many others. Can you confidently tell me that you did your job honourably?

Vladimir: (*remains silent*)

Messenger: I don't think so. You used your power to trample on those you knew couldn't defend themselves like your neighbour and extorted money from those you knew

116

were vulnerable. You were a law enforcement officer and always claimed to be representing the law. Rape was a crime you were supposed to punish but there were a good number of women under your command who came complaining of being raped by their male colleagues. You promised to do something about it but did nothing at the end of the day. Many young girls and women who lived around one of your bases came complaining to you that they had been raped and in some cases gang-raped by some of your men. You took no action. When they carried their complaints to the journalists who came to interview you, you claimed that your men were decent and honourable and could not do what they were accused of. You defended your men without first carrying out any investigations. Not taking action made you an accomplice. Those you tried to apply the law on were the poor and you applied it by making them pay money to you. Once they paid what you wanted, you released them. Added to that, you gave your weapon to armed robbers who went around terrorizing and robbing poor-innocent citizens, the same people you took an oath to protect and defend even with your life.

Vladimir: I asked them not to kill or harm anybody in the course of the operations.

Messenger: Giving instructions is one thing and those instructions being respected is quite another. You asked your friends not to kill anybody but you were never there to ensure that they carried out your instructions. Well, let me inform you that they killed, raped, cut breasts, tore open the stomachs of pregnant women and sent thousands down the road to poverty. You were not there and didn't care. All you were interested in was part of the stolen booty your friends brought to you after frustrating their victims. You who gave the orders were as guilty as they who carried out those barbaric acts. No one could be in trouble and run to you for help because you were going to find ways of getting money out of the individual who sought your protection. Yet, all those victims were people you were supposed to protect and on top of that you got promoted by your superiors. Can you tell us what happened in Delta district?

Vladimir: One of my commanders was killed there and when I sent some of my men there to go and carry out investigations, they were attacked as soon as the inhabitants spotted them. They had to defend themselves and a serious gun battle ensued in which many people were killed.

Messenger: Was that the real story or was it what you wanted people to believe? You have left out too many details there. The truth which you are afraid to say here is that most of your men were fond of supporting armed robbers, kidnappers and were in the ranks of those who committed crimes. Your commander decided not only to give weapons to some armed robbers to go and carry out a robbery in Delta District but he decided to be part of the gang. Unfortunately for him their target on the night of the operation was a well armed man who fired a shot from a hidden angle of his home. Your commander died in his yard and the well armed man dragged the body and dumped it in the street a distance further from his home. You did not send your men there to go and carry out any investigations. You sent them there to go and carry out revenge. They killed hundreds on sight and arrested many who were last seen alive only in your custody.

118

Before their deaths, you paraded them in front of TV cameras as suspected thieves and kidnappers. You treated them like condemned criminals when the law clearly stated "Innocent until proven guilty." When you were accused of extra judicial killings, you always claimed you acted within the law. Well, you could tell such lies to get away from justice down there but here, you can't escape. You must render account because everything everyman does, think or say is recorded here. That was not all about the revengeful acts you carried out. You personally went to the home of Jay Charles when he accidentally hit your kid brother with his car and he unfortunately passed away. Jay Charles presented his condolences and took total charge of the funeral program from start to finish. It was not enough to tell you that he was sorry for what he did?

Vladimir: He might have been sorry but that did not appease my family members who piled pressure on me to avenge the death of my brother because if I didn't, his soul was not going to rest in peace.

Messenger: Did it dawn on you that by carrying out revenge you were instituting a cycle of revenge? It seemed you forgot that you yourself carried out some killings. What would have happened if the families of those you killed directly or indirectly also decided to come and carry out revenge on you and your family? Did you think of the creator who created everything including you and His command concerning revenge? By carrying out the revenge, did you know that you violated your creator's fifth command? Revenge is not for you or any human but for my master alone. You preferred to please your family members and displease your creator. That was not good at all. That not withstanding, what happened on 6th April?

Vladimir: The president decided to modify the constitution to remain in power but most people in our big towns and cities were against it. They turned out in the numbers on the streets to manifest but the authorities were against it because the manifestations obstructed traffic and paralyzed businesses. That was costing the state billions and they became afraid that if the manifestations were not stopped, the government would crumble. The official version of the cause of the manifestation which the government wanted the international community to believe was that there were some individuals who wanted to seize power and were inciting the population to move out to the streets. I was asked to disperse the crowd in my town and in the course of trying to do so, many protesters were shot dead while thousands of others were arrested and imprisoned without trial.

Messenger: Did you at any one moment think that the population was being manipulated to descend to the streets?

Vladimir: No, because no one needed to incite anybody who was hungry to manifest. There was grinding poverty everywhere and a lot of inflation too.

Messenger: Were you in favour of the modification of the constitution?

Vladimir: If I became a colonel, it was thanks to those who were in power. I was gaining a lot from their system of governance. I had to be on their side.

Messenger: Do you think the people had the right to manifest?

Vladimir: The constitution made provision for that. Yes, they had the right.

Messenger: Were those manifesting in the majority or the minority?

Vladimir: Well, because of the economic hardship, most people in the villages left for the big towns and cities. On television I could see thousands in each town that television cameras went to. I think they were in the majority.

Messenger: If those who were against the revision of the constitution were in the majority, don't you think that their will should have been given a chance to prevail?

Vladimir: I think so.

Messenger: In that case, the voice of the people was the voice of my master. By refusing to listen to the voice of the people, you refused to listen to the voice of my master.

Vladimir: But I had no choice. I was just following orders. And if I didn't obey, I would have been made to face court-martial and possibly sent to prison.

Messenger: Someone is rejected by a population but you use guns to impose him on them. Someone preaches separation instead of integration and you go ahead to see to it that what he preaches is implemented. Tell me something….if you were asked to jump into a deep river when you do not know how to swim and know that if you jump in you will die, would you do it simply because it is an order?

Vladimir: I don't know.

Messenger: Of course you know. Listen, my master created everyman and endowed Him with the ability to reason. My master did not give you a brain to serve as a decoration or for you to be sleeping on. My master wanted you to act out of your freewill after making use of that brain because you were to be responsible for your actions. Have you seen any of those you took orders from here? Is any of them here to answer questions in your place or on your behalf? You are here to face your fate alone just as they will face theirs. Orders were not supposed to mar your sense of reasoning. Being a man in uniform does not mean that you would be given special considerations simply because you were trained only to take or follow orders. Do you know why? It is because the Ten Commandments were meant for everyman irrespective of race, origin or occupation. By the way, did I hear you say you had no choice? You did have a choice. You knew that those people who were manifesting were given the right to do so by the constitution and they equally had the right to vote in or vote out anybody they no longer wanted to be their leader. You had the choice to either fight by their side and by so doing disobey your superiors or to obey your superiors and slap the people in the face. You preferred to stand against the people you were supposed to defend under the pretext that you feared for your life. Well,

122

anybody who tries to save his or her life looses it and he or she who looses her life for the sake of my master gains it. My master never forgets those who undergo persecutions for His sake. Your statement to most of those you arrested and imprisoned was that "Nobody is above the state." A state can never be a land surface or the trees and rocks and animals found in it. If there were no people, there would be no state. The people make up the state and if majority rejected someone who was not supposed to be above the state, you had to stand by them. Your actions proved that your commander in chief was above the state. Is that not ironical? The truth is that you thought of only yourself and that explains why you did the things you did. You were supposed to, through your job, make yourself worthy of my master's kingdom by serving those that came to you and those that you met on your way.

Vladimir: (*Feels dejected with his head bent to the ground. Raises his head after a while*) If the people were really manipulated by some individuals who wanted to seize power, would I have been justified in intervening in the way I did?

Messenger: let's not get into conditionality. Conditionality has its place only when there is room to make amends. It is possible in that world below your feet and my master being very patient always gives everyman many chances to make amends. But amends must be made only down there. But since you've asked, I will give you an answer. I will not say if your kind of intervention would have been justified or not. But let's look at the reasons why someone would want to seize power in the first place. There could be disparities in chances between competitors. That is, the incumbent could decide to use state resources in his campaign while the other competitors get just tokens which might not be enough. The incumbent might be that one who promise a lot and delivers very little and yet want the people to continue entrusting their destinies into his hands by either constantly modifying the constitution, putting in place a sophisticated rigging machinery which rejects the choice of the people or he or she could decide to cook up reasons to sideline the other competitors who might pose as 'threats'. If rules are laid down and anybody who comes to power serves his term and at the end leaves without trying to change initial rules, there would hardly be anything like forceful take-over. Forceful take-over occurs mostly because man by nature likes to cheat. And anybody who wants to remain in power or get to power by any means possible is out not to serve the people, though they would always claim to want to serve the people. But in reality, they are out to serve themselves. But in such situations you are supposed to use your head and be on the side of justice.

Vladimir: (*In desperation*) I was just trying to serve my country and to prevent it from sinking into chaos.

Messenger: He who knows the right thing and fails to do it is as guilty as the one who consciously and out rightly does a wrong thing. If you stood by those people whom in their vast majority objected to the touching of the sacred book of their land, then you would have been serving your country. But you preferred to serve a handful of those in power who did not care about the poor and sick populace or whatever they had to say. Are you trying to make me understand that a handful of government officials became synonymous to a nation? You and I know that is not possible. Those people you dispersed, killed and imprisoned formed the nation and they were the ones you ought to serve. But no, they were not the ones you served... you served your bosses and yourself. By doing that you implemented the policy of "let the poor, the underprivileged and the unemployed die so that those in power or those who matter can survive." They reminded you and your superiors of your failure as leaders. That not withstanding, you were asked to personally execute some of the people you arrested during that unrest. Weren't you told that you were not supposed to kill?

Vladimir: I was just doing my job.

Messenger: You violated my master's fifth command in the name of doing your job? Are you telling me that you preferred human laws over the laws of my master?

Vladimir: The people I was asked to personally execute were a danger to many people and the state. They had ideas which could set the country ablaze and the only way to save the state was to eliminate such people.

Messenger: Eliminating such people was violating the fifth law of my master. As far as I know, life imprisonment behind solid iron bars can prevent any man alive from being a threat to the state if at all, the accusation is founded. Let me tell you something about crime and punishment. When my master was down there doing his evangelization mission, a woman was one day brought to him. The people who dragged the woman to my master accused her of committing adultery. The penalty for such an offense was death by stoning. The people had expected that my master would just give His accord that the woman be stoned to death but my master saw things differently. "Let he who has never committed an offense be the first to cast a stone," my master said. Nobody dared to do it and those who dragged the woman to my master started dispersing one after the other until at the end the woman was left alone. By saying that he who has never committed any offense should be the first to cast a stone, my master was asking those present to do self examination. That means that before you set out on a condemnation path, you should examine yourself first. You executed many people because they committed offenses. How were you different from them? By ordering the death of someone, supervising or carrying out the execution of someone for whatever reason, you are casting the first stone. Casting the first stone is telling the world and your creator that you've never committed any offense which is not true. By sparing the life of the adulteress, my master restored life and no man has the right to destroy it. You cannot create life and so, should not destroy it in the name of doing your job. (*A brief silence follows*) One last question; what happened between you and Hakim Willis, who was an officer under your command?

Vladimir: Why all these questions? Can't you see you are torturing me? There is no lawyer here to defend me and no witnesses here to back me up. Why do you ask me all these questions when you already know the answers?

Messenger: You do not need a lawyer or witnesses here. My master sees and knows everything. My master does not want you to feel that you have been unjustly treated and that

126

is why these questions are coming up. So, should I ask the question again?

Vladimir: Please stop torturing me.

Messenger: Ok. But I will tell you what happened between you and Willis. He had a very beautiful wife who was not working and had children to look after. One day they had an occasion and invited you. As soon as you set your eyes on his wife, you started imagining and feeling what her body could feel like. You put her in a very desperate situation by threatening to have her husband fired if she didn't comply. She thought of her jobless situation and the children she had to raise and was forced to give in. To keep her husband away, you always sent him on missions that lasted for days and weeks. Whenever Willis was away, you did whatever you pleased with his wife even though she never wanted it. Just as anything that happens under the sun and can never be hidden forever, you were caught one day when Willis returned earlier than expected. Instead of apologizing as any normal person would do in such a situation, you felt that it would be so humiliating to do so to a junior officer. You instead were insisting that he go complete his mission. A fight ensured in which you exchanged gunshots. Your shot caught him in the left shoulder while his caught you below the abdomen. You died eight minutes after the gunshot without making amends with either him or my master. That act with Willis' wife was a violation of my master's ninth commandment. Do you still feel you are unjustly kept here? Are you worthy of that kingdom over there?

Vladimir: *(Remains silent with eyes and mouth wide open as if in a trance)*

Messenger: I know it is not easy coming face to face with reality. Since you don't want to be bothered with further questions, I will tell you what happened to Ted Jennifer. She was appointed to fight against the production, sale and distribution of fake pharmaceutical products. There were a number of men who became rich and powerful thanks to the sale of the illegal and harmful drugs. Seeing that their empire was going to crumble because of the successes registered by Ted Jennifer, they waged war against her. They sent assassins to murder her and they succeeded. Your blame in that was that you were benefiting from the production, sale and distribution of the fake pharmaceutical products as those involved paid you money to allow them to do their business. Ted Jennifer was killed just a few blocks from where you were. You did not intervene and ordered your men to stay away because you had earlier been paid money and after receiving the money, you promised not to intervene. Saving people in danger was your job but you facilitated the murder of Ted Jennifer. When questioned by reporters after the incident, you claimed that things happened very fast and you were not aware of what was happening a few blocks from where you stood. The reporters had no choice but to believe what you said because they were humans. Here you cannot tell such lies because the evidence would be played before your eyes. You were as guilty as those involved in the sale of the fake drugs as well as the assassins. However, there is one more thing I have to tell you before I take my leave. What I have to say concerns my master. One day when He was down there in that world where you've just come from doing His teaching mission, a man walked up to him. "What must I do to gain eternal life?" the man asked. My master gave him some scriptures and they were the Ten Commandments. "I have followed all those scriptures my whole life," the man said. My master admired and praised him for that and told him that there was still something lacking. When the man sought to know what the missing thing in his life was, my master told him that he had go and sell everything he owned and give the money to the poor and after doing that he should come and follow Him (my master). The man went away very disappointed because he was a very wealthy man. Do you know why the man went away disappointed? It was because he was too attached to his wealth and could not imagine himself living a life of poverty. That is to tell all of you here that respecting the Ten Commandments and being religious are not enough. Those two are just stepping stones to the kind of life that leads to eternal life. You have to associate action to the respect of the commandments and being religious. The action my master wanted the man to associate was using just a small fraction of his wealth to buy clothes for those that were naked, buy food for the hungry, buy some medicine for the sick,…. In short, little acts of charity. But the man got disappointed and did not want to include action to his religious life which in effect was service to humanity. Almost all of you here went to prayer houses and knew the commandments. You had to associate that 'service to humanity part' or action part to it through the posts of responsibility you all occupied. Did you serve humanity? You start preparing for eternal life when other people's problems become a preoccupation to you and you help them find solutions to them. That is associating action to your religious life.

(Exit Messenger)
Curtain.

Scene 2: (The gate opens and someone walks in. He is met at the gate by the Messenger)

Cain: *(To the messenger)* are you the luggage carrier? I'm afraid there is no luggage to carry.

Messenger: I'm no luggage carrier. I'm a messenger.

Cain: A messenger? Whose messenger?

Messenger: I work for the one who made everything that you knew in that world below as well as all what you can see here.

Cain: I know who that is. Down there He was referred to as The Most High, Creator, Supreme Being, … He had many names. But wait a minute, I was told that up here there were beautiful flowers, trees of all sorts, animals and birds living next to one another without being afraid, …quite a lot of nice things. But I see none here. I guess all those preachers just had their heads in the clouds.

Messenger: Maybe…..maybe not.

(As they walk by the rooms of Carlos and Vladimir)

Cain: *(To messenger)* Look, those guys in those two room don't look ok. What's wrong with them? Are they sick?

Messenger: Sort of.

Cain: Then I think I might be of help. I was a medical doctor down there. But I wonder if they would have the money to pay for my services. I am expensive and very conscious of it. When I was down there, I dealt only with the rich. Anyone who came to me and claimed to be poor was sent elsewhere or if they remained begging, they ended up dying.

Messenger: But I thought that when you are a medical doctor, your first priority was to save lives and not bother whether they are rich or poor.

Cain: Well, yes….but that was the ideal and nobody liked the ideal. You know, I came from a modest family and I was not bright in school. So my parents used money to push me through schools and bought me certificates. Towards the end of my third year in the university, there were no prospects of ever finding a job. My parents still had to dip their hands really deep into their pockets to buy my way into the medical school. They went in for a loan and assembled six million which they paid. It did not end there….since I was not bright they still had to keep bribing the lecturers to give me good marks until I finally graduated. When I started work, I had to repay all the money they spent. I thought that after repaying the money, I would stop. But that was not the case. I soon discovered how it was so easy to make money from patients and my appetite for it became insatiable. I began to have numerous girlfriends, good cars, beautiful houses, long travels to towns and cities that had sandy beaches….the list is long. Life was good down there. You can now understand why I made mention of money. Money is good.

Messenger: I see….I don't think those guys would be in need of your services. What they are suffering from is some depression which will disappear with the passage of time. You know, time heals all wounds. But I think you would soon have to doctor yourself as you will have the depression too.

Cain: (*Stops and looks startled*) What do you mean I will soon have a depression? Is there a depression epidemic around here?

Messenger: Yes. It grips people when they learn of the truth and you know that the truth hurts and leads to depression. But don't worry about it….since you are a doctor, I'm sure you are well armed to face the situation. Can I show you to your room?

(*They enter the room intended for him. It is as empty as the rest. Cain looks around the room with a lot of curiosity*).

Cain: Is this the room you talked about or another one?

Messenger: This is the room….your room.

Cain: This? There is no chair or table or cooking pot or anything….how am I supposed to survive here? Is there nothing better than this? Who is in charge of this place by the way? If I see him I'd tell him in his face that this place is below standards.

Messenger: I can see that you don't like this place but you are the one who willingly made the choice to come here.

Cain: Me? Choose to come here? What are you talking about?

Messenger: A while ago you told me that preachers painted a very beautiful picture of the place good people go to after death, right?

Cain: Yes, I said that.

Messenger: They didn't tell you what you had to do to get there?

Cain: They did but what they were telling me to do was too difficult. They wanted me to forgo all the beautiful things of life. They equally added that I had to sacrifice a good chunk of what I earned by giving it to charity as well as treat most of those that were poor, who came to me, free of charge. One of the preachers went as far as telling me that I had to use part of my salary to buy drugs for some of my patients who could not afford it. Those things were too difficult to follow. If I did it I wouldn't have enjoyed my life.

Messenger: The picture of the beautiful place they painted really does exist. I'm equally sure they told you that the road to the place is rough and narrow. What makes the road rough and narrow are the temptations of that world which you call pleasure and a good life. Willing to forgo them meant that you had to be at constant war with yourself. Battling those things which your heart and body desired most was the way you were supposed to prepare yourself for the place they painted as beautiful. You said that following what they prescribed was difficult and so you sunk into that life of vanity or nothingness. By doing that, you were preparing for the life of nothingness and you are in the land of nothingness. Do you want to know where that beautiful place is? (*Pointing*) Look over there... that is the place.

Cain: So what is this place?

Messenger: Do you want to tell me you weren't listening. I've said (*pointing*) that is the Land of Eternal Happiness over there while this one is the opposite side.

Cain: What can I do to get there?

Messenger: What can you do to get there? Well right now....nothing. While you were in that world down there, you were supposed to send something for us out of that world to prepare a place for you. But you didn't do that.

Cain: Now wait a minute, how was I supposed to send money here for you to build me a good house when you don't even have financial institutions here?

Messenger: I didn't say anything about money. Besides, money is not needed here no matter the amount. What was required to prepare you a place here was resistance of those good things of life down there, service to humanity through your job especially the poor, help for those who couldn't help themselves, charity to the poor and love for every man no matter the status, class, sex or origin. That was all that was needed to prepare a place for you over there. Now that you sent nothing, nothing was prepared for you there and there is nothing which you have to go and do there. That difficult path the preachers prescribed actually led to that beautiful place but since you felt it was too difficult, this is where your path has led you. I will be out for a while but will be back to clarify any doubts you may have. Losing you was already too painful for my master just as all those who are here. He wouldn't want you to feel that you are in this place unjustly as well.

(Exit Messenger)

Cain: Ok. (*Does not look convinced. Jumps out and heads to Vladimir's room where William, Stone, and Sandi are seated on the bare floor. Bumps in. without greeting and almost in tears*) Please I need some help. I am just a new comer here and that guy who calls himself a messenger has told me a lot of things which are pretty scary. Can any of you explain what he said?

William: (*Very calmly*) Sure boy….what do you want to know?

Cain: (*Nervously*) He told me that He who created us has already lost those of us that are here and that we have no place in that beautiful kingdom over there because we do not merit a place there. Is that true?

William: Didn't he tell you who he is? He is a Messenger of the one who created everything including all of us here. If he has said anything to you, you have to take it as the whole truth because when it comes to knowing the number of teeth

136

in a crocodile's mouth, you are not supposed to argue with the fish.

Sandi: Just to add to what he has said, if that gate opened to let you in, it means that you are supposed to be here and once you get in here, you can never get out again. That is what I have learnt to my finger tips and I think you should do the same thing.

Cain: Is that all what he told you guys? How do you know he was speaking the truth?

Stone: Because some of us tried to get out and failed. That Messenger is the only one who can come in here and get out again. If that is not enough evidence to you, then find those that suit you.

Cain: So what is this place?

Sandi: It is called the Land of Eternal Discomfort or Hell if you want.

Cain: (*Raises both hands to his head and crashes to the ground*).

(*Enters Messenger*)

Messenger: (*To Cain*) I told you that you were going to suffer a depression. Given the situation in which you are, I will not bother you with many questions. But I will ask you just one and then point out why you are here. My first question is; do you think that you are in this place unjustly?

Cain: I admit that I did a few terrible things but I don't think they were enough to land me here.

Messenger: Let's try to examine what you call 'few'. At your post of duty, you carried out surgical operations which had nothing to do with your field of study at school. You were actually or should I say presumably trained to be a general practitioner. I say presumably because you were not a bright student and your parents bribed the lecturers to give you good marks. You just had to prescribe drugs. But since the prescription of drugs was not lucrative, you forcefully decided to carry out surgical operations since there was a lot of money to be made. Your principal targets were pregnant women about to give birth. You took upon yourself to always program their minds to know that giving birth naturally was no longer possible. Your first victim was Anastasia Lee. You made her believe that her baby was too fat and would kill her if she gave birth normally. You charged 150.000 and operated on her to take out a baby who weighed just two and a half kilograms. She could have given birth naturally. You successfully took out the baby but on stitching her wounds you forgot some pads in her which later rendered her sterile. Another victim was Juliana. You charged the same 150.000 as soon as she entered your office already in labour. After collecting the money, you went to prepare the theatre and on returning, she had given birth. You did not refund her money. So far, have I said anything which is out of place?

Cain: (*Remains silent*).

Messenger: That silence means that all I've said is in order. Catherine was yet another victim. She actually needed an operation to give birth but her crime was that she was poor. What you did….

Cain: (*Interrupts*) What happened to her was not my responsibility. She did not have the money to pay and I could not operate on her. She had the choice to either go and look for the money or call her relatives to come and take her elsewhere.

Messenger: You did not sound like you were giving her a choice. You told her family members to go and look for money. They were not just going to look for your initial fee but they had to equally provide money for drugs which you were the only one to provide and administer. Did they really have a choice?

Cain: But I ended up not operating on her since I was incompetent as you've said. Haven't you just said that I had nothing to do with surgery? So by not intervening, I did her a lot of good.

Messenger: I am not the one saying it. You yourself knew that you had nothing to do with surgery yet you went on practicing it. If not intervening was good for Catherine, she wouldn't have died, would she? Are you then telling me that if her family members did come with the money, you wouldn't have carried out the operation? You would have done it. Because of your love for money, you allowed Catherine to die with her twin babies. She was not the only one who suffered that fate. Most of the women you operated on ended up dying and those that survived were those who went for surgical interventions elsewhere.

Cain: So why am I here? Is it because jobs were rare and I found myself in the one that was available which of course I didn't like?

Messenger: You must not like a job before carrying it out properly. Anyone who has the desire to do things right, and the will to learn, will always do the job he or she is in, even if he or she does not like the job. Well back at school, you did not want to learn because you knew your parents were going to bribe the lecturers to get you promoted. You were fully aware that it was the 'Only available Job' as you put it. That was supposed to be a galvanizer to make you develop love, dedication, determination and devotion to the profession. That is, saving lives. It is a divine ordination. The fact that you did not love your job was not reason to turn the hospital into a slaughter house. You did not love the job but loved the money generated by the job.

Cain: You are here blaming me alone leaving out my parents who decided to use money in getting me into school and bribing lecturers, and lecturers who were too corrupt and accepted money to award me marks which I did not merit. What about them? Let's even say that I operated on Catherine for free, where would have the money for her drugs come from?

Messenger: As for your parents and the corrupt lecturers, they have their case files which they would come and face. Going back to Catherine, she died in the afternoon of the same day Juliana gave birth. Juliana gave birth in the morning and paid you 150.000 plus that for her drugs. If she had the choice to go out to the hospital pharmacy to buy her drugs, they would have cost only half of the amount you charged her. You still had the money on you at the time Catherine died and the drugs she would have needed after the operation were equally available. Why didn't you use them to save her life?

Cain: What? I should have used my hard earned money or drugs to save her life for free!!! Who was she to me? She was nobody....a total stranger.

Messenger: That is what I've been saying all along. Was there any other way of testing your dedication to the life-saving mission? Your love for money prevented you from seeing her as a patient, sister and human being who needed assistance. You convinced her and she came to you because she had faith in you. If you were in that job, whether you liked it or not, your principal mission was to save lives whether the patient was rich or poor. If you discovered that you had some lapses, nothing stopped you from inviting or asking assistance from your colleagues who were specialists. You could not because you were afraid of sharing part of the charges you made with them. Because of your greed and selfishness, many patients paid dearly with their lives. That was not all....your boss received a lot of criticisms because of the chronic corruption which went on in the hospital and decreed that all consultation fees must be paid in a special office he created. You still charged consultation fees even after your patients presented receipts showing that they had already paid. As a medical practitioner you were not allowed to sell drugs and there were notices all over the hospital premises prohibiting doctors and nurses from selling drugs. Yet you ignored them (sentence not clear).

Cain: Those who wrote such notices were still selling drugs as well.

Messenger: You were gaining a lot from the illegal sale of drugs but you were at the same time crippling the patient. It was not because those who wrote the notices violated them that you had to do the same. You developed the habit of sending your patients to the lab even when you knew what was wrong with them and knew the drug to prescribe.

Cain: I had to send them to the lab to be sure that I wasn't prescribing the wrong drug for the wrong disease. Through those tests, we could identify other diseases the patients were not aware of.

Messenger: I did not say that sending your patients to the lab was wrong. But the intention for sending them there was not proper. You had arranged with the lab technicians to be collecting money which they shared equally with you. As proof that you were interested more in making money, tests conducted had to be prepaid whether they turned out positive or negative. For people who were interested in saving lives, the right thing would have been to conduct all tests and then the patients pay just for those that turn out positive. That would have been better and would have helped to save lives. But since you were more interested in making money, you fixed an amount first and patients had to pay first before any tests were conducted. You drained money from your patients by making them undergo tests which turned out to be negative and by the time you got to what they were actually suffering from, they no longer had money for drugs, which sent a good number of them to their graves. Such behaviour made many believe that the hospital was a money making institution which contributed to the killing of patients who went there seeking treatment. You inflated the prices of the drugs which you were not allowed to sell in the first place because you knew that people must buy to stay alive. You took advantage of some scarcity to inflate the prices. My master frowns at those who take advantage of desperate situations. Where did you keep your compassion? Even at this moment we are talking, the hospitals especially state run hospitals are big money making institutions. Using people for whatever reason for self benefit is wrong and failing to help or save someone in difficulties especially in a life and death situation is as bad as physically killing him or her. Can you tell us what happened to Luanga Thompson?

Cain: He was an immigrant who came into my country under the pretext that he was running away from insecurity back in his own home country. He made up a story that men in uniform came to his village and killed many people on sight, raped their women and burnt down their villages. Those were the stories many foreigners who came to my country narrated. I believed such stories were just cooked up. The real reason why they left their countries and were flooding mine was in search of a better life. I had no problem with them seeking a better life but they would have gone elsewhere. I was not happy with those supposed refugees because they were stealing our jobs and accepting lower salaries for jobs offered to them. As a result, employers mostly employed them leaving my indigenous brothers and sisters jobless.

Messenger: You still have not said what happened to Luanga.

Cain: I got frustrated by the influx of foreigners and thought that it was better for them to be repatriated or killed if they did not want to go back willingly. I….(Pauses) I….(Pauses)

Messenger: You have some problems saying what happened to Luanga. I will help you there. Since you did not like foreigners, you wanted some of them dead. You took advantage of the fact that Luanga fell sick and came to you for medical attention to imprison him in a ward and allowed him to die unattended to. As I said before, your primary mission in that hospital was to save lives and the origin of those who came to you for medical attention was not supposed to be an issue. Now tell me…do you know what happened to you before you came here?

Cain: It was the husband of one of the women who died in my theatre room who injected me with some poison. He held me responsible for what happened to his wife.

Messenger: The poison was the venom of a serpent. You couldn't survive but you were given a few hours. You had to go through agony and in that agony, see my Master's face and make amends for the terrible life you led. But in those few dark hours, you did not see my master's face. What you concentrated on were the material things you were going to miss if you ended up dead. You saw only the face of money. (To all) Money has come between my master and His flock. That is why He blessed everything except money. It is

144

the root of all evil. All of you here deviated from your missions because of money. You became mean and heartless for its sake. (To Cain) You went on the internet and posed as a business man and duped a couple in a foreign country of $1000.000.00 which was what they had laboured for all their lives. Did you bother to know what became of that couple? Did you bother to think of your creator's command on coveting your neighbour's goods?

Do you still consider all what I have brought out as insignificant few which did not warrant your coming here? If you still think so, I will point out more that you did outside the hospital premises.

Cain: (*Remains silent*).

Messenger: My master is a just Master and you wouldn't be here if you couldn't be here. You are here because you did things which you were not supposed to do and after doing those things, my master in His compassion still decided to give you a last chance which you deliberately refused to take advantage of. What did you do with all the money you collected from your patients? You spent it in beer parlours and hotels with free girls and women. That was your life.

(*Messenger exits and moves towards the gate*)

Scene 3: Still in Vladimir's room

William: (*To Cain*) Listening to what you did, I feel some relief as somewhere deep within me a voice tells me that my case was better. What are some of the other things you did that the Messenger did not want to talk about?

Cain: (*With a stern look, does not say anything*).

William: I'm sure that if any of those book makers who love telling stories were here to listen to your deeds down there, they would go back and produce encyclopaedias. Your case is really heavy. (*The rest burst into laughter including Cain*) jokes aside.... We were all businessmen while we were down there. What I mean is that we had different occupations but in practical terms, we were businessmen.

Stone: I was a businessman in the true sense of the word. That was really my occupation.

Sandi: I was no business man.

William: Ah yes.....you were the religious soldier-dreamer. But the rest of us turned the places we were into business premises when we were not supposed to. We are just reaping the fruits of our labour now. We deserve what is happening to us. We did not do the right thing and this is the price for failing to do the right thing. Why don't we go and see how Carlos is doing? He has not left his room ever since he learnt that he could not go back to his palace.

Stone: I think that is a good idea.

(*They all exit except Cain*)

Scene 4: In Carlos' Room (Enter William, Stone and Sandi. Carlos watches them with a surprised look on his face)

William: Hi Sir, we have come to find out how you are doing.

Carlos: You have just addressed me as Sir and that means that you know me.

William: That is true. I was your loyal subject down there. You could not know me since I worked more with the minister of justice down there. I helped to send most of those people who were a threat to you either to prison or to the grave.

Carlos: Were you a uniform officer?

William: No Sir. I was one of the masters of the law.

Carlos: So you are a master of the law and you couldn't say anything in my defence when that Messenger was tormenting me with all those very challenging questions?

William: But Sir, you were head of the judiciary while we were down there and by the normal trend of happenings or stratification, anybody at the head must be better than his or her subordinates. With that in mind, I said nothing, knowing that you could better defend yourself without me. Besides, you decided what was right or wrong or what punishment anyone was subjected to while we were down there.

Carlos: That is where you are wrong. I might be better than you in status but not in matters of the law. I did not go to any law school though I made myself head of the judiciary and passed sentences on those I saw as enemies. Is there anything I wasn't made the head of?

William: I'm sure you can now see why the people always wanted the judiciary to be independent. There was no need saying anything to defend you since we are all condemned.

Carlos: That is the problem with this place. No one can hire a lawyer and they know everything.
(*Brief silence*) all I ever wanted was to serve my people and to continue serving them.

William: Sir, I don't think the word 'Serve' is an appropriate one to describe what you really wanted and did. Anybody who wants to serve does not need to do so with the use of force or fraud. Of course the people are the meat in every politician's soup. They always claim they want to serve the people when in reality they are out to serve themselves. No servant would want to serve using force. Are you sure you really wanted to serve the people?

Carlos: On which side are you? Are you here to criticize me or to support me?

William: I am here on my side. I am trying to help you come to terms with your deeds. The earlier that happens, the better for you. Do you like the state of mind in which you find yourself now?

Carlos: What do you want to tell me?

William: What I want to say is that before you became president, there were others before you. They helped put in place laws after concerting with the people. They respected those laws because they were actually out to serve. When you came and after serving your two terms which were catastrophic, you refused to go. You wanted to change those laws which your predecessors put in place and respected. Most of the people were against it but you unleashed the uniform officers on them. What did you still want to prove that you couldn't during your two terms of office? If you were really out to serve, you would have respected the wish of the people and stepped aside. The truth is that you were there to serve yourself. As proof, you built a very magnificent palace for yourself. You spent most of your time in the rich countries in very luxurious hotels. In most of your trips, you had an entourage of sometimes more than 40 men and they had to lodge with you in the same hotel. The least time you spent on any of your trips was a week. The amount you had to pay for your hotel bills was the equivalent of 30 million of our local currency per day. Calculate all that for the two weeks and sometimes three months you spent out and then multiply by the number of times you went out. Can you tell us here a real figure? I don't think so. That was not out of your salary....it was the tax payer's money you went spending lavishly like that. Yet there were millions who survived on less than a dollar a day as the human rights campaigners always said. You tasted power and saw that it was sweet and you wanted to remain there. It was wrong....very wrong.

Carlos: What do you mean by my two terms being catastrophic?

William: What I mean is that during your term in office, more people did not get jobs. Instead, thousands sunk down into poverty. You kept telling the population that the money they contributed went to pay debts incurred by your predecessors but that was not true. You and I know that. If you were actually paying debts, you would have come out with figures showing how much debt there was, how much was paid and how much was left to be paid. None of that ever happened. The money was going into your numerous private bank accounts. In addition, over taxing forced many companies out of business which caused many layoffs and no companies were allowed to come in, unless they agreed to surrender a percentage of their profit to you. That scared many who went elsewhere. You thought that the only way to make the people worship you was to keep them poor. Trying to change the constitution was the worst thing to have thought of.

Carlos: If I wanted to change the constitution, it was because majority of the people were behind me. Each time I said I was going to visit an area, they came out in their numbers to welcome me and they did so in songs. They might have been poor but they loved me.

William: That was not true. Is it because they came out chanting songs and some smiled with you that you felt they loved you? They were being forced to do so. In the localities where your visit was announced, principals of schools were forced to suspend lessons so that the learners would come

152

out to sing praise songs which you loved so much. Business men were forced to close down their businesses until you came and left. Some people were forced out of their homes to come and listen to you. Your special guards were the ones going around and forcing people. Your visits helped in starving some people because their businesses were disrupted. If everybody was free to choose whether to come and see you or not, you would have known that the people no longer wanted you. They had nothing to benefit from your visits. The people never loved you. That is a fact. They were being forced to come and you can't tell me that you didn't know that the people were being forced. You wanted the international community to give you some credibility.

Carlos: I disagree with you.

William: Whether you agree or not is no longer important. You are already condemned. You know that down there, we always said that politics is a dirty game. I think it is true in all the facets of the term. It is really dirty and this is where the dirtiness has landed us. Down there we saw it really as a game and permitted all rules so long as one used them to achieve his or her goals. We can fidget and get away with any atrocities in our course to attain power down there but once we cross that bar which separates this world from that one, we will be held accountable. No lawyers are needed here. I didn't need to say anything in your defence. They know everything even before you think of an idea to when you execute it. They know things even before they happen. If that messenger asked you any questions, it is not that he didn't know the answer. He just wanted you to point out your wrong doing yourself. If you refused to speak, he would have told you what you did. Our rules trampled on those of our Creator. We were supposed to understand that our creator shall always be the ultimate destination for every man. We therefore had to use His rules to shape those that we put in place to govern ourselves. That was where we failed and are now paying the price. I supported you in that game and went around telling people that everything in the country was well. I did not care about the plight of the poor who were in their millions. I saw things only from my perspective. Since I was fine, I went around generalizing that the whole country was fine. I knew the reality on the ground but supported what was wrong and professed lies. That was one of the points in my case file. I served myself and saw that life down there more beautiful than the one I would have had in that golden city (*pointing*) over there. Things have turned out this way to teach us that you can get into the House of Representatives through the back door or use money to buy your way into any high office but you cannot buy your way into that golden city. Nevertheless, I would like to end with a story which was told by a preacher when my friend Augustus died and was taken to a house of prayer for the last requiem.

Sandi: (*Interrupts*) Was it a true story or a made up one?

William: Whether it was a true story or not is not very important. What matters is the lesson we can learn from it. As I was saying, after the first and second readings, the gospel came next. The preacher began his homily with the story which I want to tell you now. "There was a king who had four wives," he began. "He did not marry all of them at the same time. He married his first wife when he was still very young and the second, when he was older and the third, when he was much older and the fourth, when he was old. There came a time when he knew he would die and decided to go round to ask all his wives if they would accompany him on the journey beyond. He began with his fourth wife. "I have loved you with all my heart and given everything you could possibly dream or imagine for the short time you have been with me. I now feel that my days down here are numbered and I was wondering if you would like to accompany me on my journey to the world beyond," he said. The fourth wife in response said that there was no way she would accompany him because she was still very young and beautiful and still had enough time to pick up another man and continue with her life. Her answer to him was a vehement 'No". The king was very disappointed and went to his third wife with the same request in the hope that he would get some consolation. He was mistaken as his third wife told him that she was young and already belonged to someone else. That answer from his third wife shattered his heart into pieces and frustration enveloped him. He went to his second wife hoping to have an answer that could take away the pain caused by his fourth and third wives. He presented his request and the second wife accepted to follow him but her acceptance had some conditions attached. She accepted to follow him only for a short distance. It was a little consoling but not enough. So, he went to his first wife and presented his request. She responded "I have been the one who has loved you truly through these years. I have loved you in the good and the bad times. Yet I was the one who suffered most from your abandonment and years of neglect in the cold as you married more women after me. I have always loved you and you know that. I will go with you anywhere you want me to go.". With those words, the king fell down at the feet of his first wife and begged for forgiveness amidst tears streaming down his face. Now, all of us are like that king who was married to four wives. Our fourth wife is our body. We do everything possible to keep it young and beautiful using all sorts of cosmetics. But that body does not belong to us. It belongs to the earth. It will abandon us when we are in desperate need. Yet, it is the one we struggle to please most. We steal, rob, extort, dupe and do anything for money to use in pleasing our fourth wives. We join sects and offer human sacrifices for the sake of our first wives. We cling to power because of the advantages that go with it. Such advantages only go to satisfy the body which does not belong to us. Our thirds wives are our wealth and all the material things we spend our lives amassing. When we die, we do not take any along. When we die, our wealth belongs to other people and that is why our third wives cannot come with us. Our second wives are our family, friends and relatives. They are the ones who would accept to accompany us for a short distance. The grave side is where they would end. Our first wife is our soul and it is the one we always neglect. It is with us from the moment we are conceived and it is with us even beyond the grave. We are all here because we neglected our first wives right to the last hour and minute. Instead we spent our lives amassing wealth and money to please our second, third and fourth wives who would abandon us at the end. I'm sure that you must be convinced beyond every reasonable doubt that you are where you chose to be.

Act Five

Scene 1: Messenger and Common man enter the room he is to occupy for the time being.

Messenger: This is the room you would be occupying for a short while.

Common Man: This place is very hot. Down there where I came from, only some people called Arabs lived in such hot places. I always wondered how they coped in such places. Maybe they were made with special brushes.

Messenger: Indeed, they were not the only ones made with special brushes. Everyman was made with a special brush because my master made everybody with love.

Common Man: (*Observes the environment around and finds only dryness every where. Thinks for a while and then jumps as if suddenly awoken from slumber by a strange noise. Looks very worried.*) What is this place? Let it not be that place that the preachers warned us about. Please just tell me that it is not.

Messenger: I wish I could tell you it is not. Let's first of all examine the kind of life you led down there before concluding. That is the best way to proceed.

Common Man: (*Calms down a little.*) I think you are right.

Messenger: Ok. You went to the house of prayer a lot and you talked of a place the preachers warned you about. Did the preachers tell you what you had to do to avoid that place?

Common Man: Yes.

Messenger: Did you follow their prescriptions?

Common Man: I did my utmost best.

Messenger: Let's see what your utmost best was. You went to the house of prayer and was told that you were not supposed to have any master other than the one talked about in that House of prayer. Did you obey that?

Common Man: (*Remains silent*)

Messenger: You went to a soothsayer and collected some things which you believed protected you. You carried such things under your garments and went to the house of prayer to listen to the prescriptions of the preachers. Do you think my master's power was not powerful enough to protect you?

Common Man: It is not that I had doubts but there were a lot of good people I knew that suffered terrible fates. There was Thomas who could not even hurt an ant. Someone killed a person and came and hid the murder weapon behind the house of Thomas. He was arrested, tried and sentenced to death. Where was the Almighty the preachers talked about? There was also Jessica. She was fondly called the mother of children because of the special care and love she gave to children especially orphans. She died in a fatal car accident. Where was the Almighty when the only hope for those parentless children was taken away by death? In addition, Pamela had a misunderstanding with a neighbour over a piece of land. Her neighbour warned her not to ever set foot on the said land. The neighbour went to a soothsayer and got some charms which he brought back and buried in the land in question. Pamela believed only in the sky and met her doom the day she stepped in that contested piece of land. Where was the Almighty she believed in? Why did He allow such terrible things to happen to such good people? More over, I had enemies who were trying to harm me using charms gotten from soothsayers. I had to use the weapons they employed to fight back. Those are some of the things that pushed me to seek an option B protection.

Messenger: When calamity strikes in any society or community, both the good and the bad people suffer. When rain comes, it falls on the roofs of the good and the bad. The same thing happens with sunshine. There are no fates reserved only for the good or only for the bad. You were told that my master is the only giver and taker of life. Letting the good people go through terrible fates as you call it, is the path chosen by my master for them to use in coming back home and you are not supposed to question His ways. You cannot serve two masters at a time. You had to either serve the soothsayer or my master. That aside, do you remember Achilles Wolf?

Common Man: Yes I do. He was a very good man and it is terrible what happened to him.

Messenger: What happened to him?

Common Man: He was arrested, tried and sentenced to death for committing high treason. He was accused of being a

161

spy working for an enemy state. The truth was that he was too vocal and condemned the government for its bad governance, poor human right records, chronic corruption, rampant embezzlement and huge unemployment rate. The government became too uncomfortable with his criticisms which he did even on foreign media. He had to put aside at all cost.

Messenger: Haven't you left out some important details?

Common Man: That was what happened to Achilles.

Messenger: You are right when you say that the government wanted him eliminated. The government bought some witnesses to come and testify against Achilles and you were one of them. You testified that you saw him conversing and giving out vital information to some foreigners. You helped in sending him to the grave. In the house of prayer, you were warned against bearing false witness. It was punishable by the law of the state and by divine law preached in the houses of prayer. When you were giving false testimony, what were you thinking?

Common Man: It was the government that asked me to say what I said. They offered me money which I knew I would never have had in my whole lifetime. It would have been insane to be in serious financial problems and then turn down such an offer.

Messenger: So, because of money, you sold a human being like yourself. What happened to the love for others preached in the house of prayer you attended?

162

Common Man: I was just trying to survive. It was not my intention to contribute to the shedding of the blood of that man.

Messenger: But you did. Tell me something; what happened on Feb 8th?

Common Man: Violence broke out following the proclamation of election results. There were some people who were not happy with the results proclaimed.

Messenger: Did the results reflect the will of the people?

Common Man: The results were free, fair and very transparent. Those who started the violence were just sore losers. They were doing it in bad fate, all with the intention to discredit the candidate who was declared as winner.

Messenger: A while ago, you talked of Achilles being killed because he criticized a government that was corrupt, noted for having bad human rights records and bad governance and so on. Could such a government be trusted to organizing free and fair elections?

Common Man: I don't know but nothing stops such a government from doing so.

Messenger: That was a very technical answer. You've just talked of the elections which were free and fair. If you can remember, you would confirm that during campaigns before voting, you went around distributing food and money to people who were pushed to the wall by the hard life the inappropriate policies of the government subjected them to. A good number of them could neither read nor write and you promised them more if they voted for the candidate you showed them. If I say something which is out of place, please feel free to stop me. On the Election Day proper, you were in charge of a polling station and you stuffed the boxes in your charge with the ballot papers of your candidate. You faked the signatures of those you were supposed to work with. You paid a good number of youths to go around doing multiple voting in favour of your own candidate. You promised money to those who went into the polling stations and came out with the ballot papers of opponents. What was free and fair about all that? The government you helped to maintain in power was already too unpopular. Do you know what doing that meant? You helped spark the clashes during which many people were killed. By doing that you frustrated the will of the people. He who frustrates the will of the people frustrates the will of my master. He who stuffs ballot boxes frustrates the will of my master. He who inflates or tampers with real election results frustrates the will of the people and the will of my master. He who carries out multiple voting, sidelines the will of the people and the will of my master. In everything that every man does, he must let the will of my master prevail first. In those elections, you relegated the will of my master to the background in favour of that of your candidate. So far, have I said anything which is out of proportion?

Common Man: No.

Messenger: Good. You were the head of your community and financial aid was given for you to construct a bridge and a water point where poor members of your

164

community could get potable drinking water. Did you use the money the way it was supposed to be used?

Common Man: (*Stammering*) I---I built the—the bridge and---and ---and constructed the water point.

Messenger: You did construct the bridge and the water point. You sliced a good chunk of the money and put in your pocket after corrupting to be awarded the contract. The bridge was constructed using inadequate and substandard materials. It gave way just four months after it was opened. The water point at least was well constructed. The inhabitants were supposed to carry potable water there free of charge. But you imposed a fee claiming that it was meant for maintenance. The local council was taking care of the maintenance and treatment of the water. Were you really doing any maintenance?

Common Man: I needed money and I was just trying to survive.

Messenger: Well, everything you do has a reward no matter how small or how big. Being in need is no reason to be dishonest. That aside, who was Ricardo to you?

Common Man: He was a poor boy I employed to help do some little jobs, in and around the house.

Messenger: Did you treat him nicely?

Common Man: I must confess that I did not treat him nicely. He came to my country with legal documents but after some months, they got expired and he did not want to go back to his country because conditions there were very bad. Having expired documents meant that he could not apply for any legal jobs. So, he had to work in hiding to survive. I asked him to work in and around my house for one and a half years. I told him that I would pay him only at the end of the one year and a half. I made him believe that it was better for me to gather money and give him in bulk so that he could do something better with it rather than getting a little amount at the end of each month. I fed him once in a while.

Messenger: Did you keep your promise to pay him in one year and a half?

Common Man: No.

Messenger: When the one and a half years came to an end and he came for his money, you refused to pay and asked him to disappear before you called the immigration police to come and arrest and deport him. Do you know what it is to work for one and half years without pay? Did you at any time try to fit yourself in that poor young man's position? What you did was inhumane. If you pleaded with him to work for you without pay, that would have been something different. But you promised to pay and at the end did not. That is called exploitation and slavery.

Common Man: I'm sorry.

Messenger: You should have said that to Ricardo and not me. There was this young footballer called Sebastian. What happened to him?

Common Man: (*Remains silent*).

Messenger: Haven't you heard the question? Should I ask it again?

Common Man: (*Exasperatedly*) No, no, I've heard the question….there is no need to ask it again.

Messenger: So?

Common Man: He was a talented young man in the art of football and I…I….I….

Messenger: Let me help you. He was a talented footballer and saw the game as the only route to escape the excruciating poverty he found himself in. He developed dreams of playing in one of the top football clubs in any of the wealthier countries, which was quite normal. What you did was that you posed as an agent having links to many of the top clubs who could sign a very juicy contract with him. You knew that was what he wanted to hear and you tricked him and his family to part with all the money and possessions they had in the whole world. Once you had everything in your hands, you told him that you were going to travel to a neighbouring country with him and from there, he would board a flight bound for the land of his dreams. Once in that neighbouring country, you abandoned him at the airport with no money, food, passport or visa. Have you ever bothered to learn what happened to him or what became of his family?

Common Man: (*remains silent*)

Messenger: How would you have felt if someone had done the same thing to you? What you did what an intentional and well calculated act. Your intention was to get money while at the same time crippling your victim. In the eyes my master, that was very disdainful and do you know why? It was because that act was a direct violation of the 7th and 10th commandments. Now tell me, what was your relationship with your tenants?

Common Man: I was really unfortunate with the kind of tenants that kept coming to rent my houses. They kept complaining of the bills that I personally handed to them to pay. My tenants did not like me much. I thought I was doing them a favour by allowing them to rent my houses instead of the streets. But they hated me and I did not understand why.

Messenger: They did not hate you because you gave them bills. They hated you because you pushed all the bills to them including yours. You used electricity and water as you pleased in your own apartment. When the water and the electricity companies brought their bills, you took them and did not allow any of your tenants to see, even after protests. You then wrote figures on pieces of papers which when put together were far above what was written on the company bills and then gave them to your tenants. After collecting and taking out the original amount on the company bills, you then kept the rest as profit for yourself. Some of your tenants knew that was what you were doing and that was the reason why they did not like your actions. You would still tell me that you were just trying to survive if I ask you, right? By the way, who was Jennifer Jeanne to you and what happened to her?

Common Man: Why do you keep asking me questions which you know the answers? Is it intended to torture me?

Messenger: I'm only asking you questions. They are not intended to punish you. You are right when you say that I know the answers to the questions I ask. Well, I will say the answer to that last question. Jennifer was your wife and you maltreated her in so many ways. First you dated her best friend and neglected her when she was pregnant. You pushed her by your infidelity and brutality to develop high blood pressure. You did not even go to see her in the hospital the day she gave birth to your second son. She returned home and was suffering alone with her children while you were having a nice time with her best friend. She died in the house alone out of too much thinking coupled with high blood pressure. How could you subject your other half to such a treatment?

Common Man: I'm so sorry.

Messenger: Since you were the head of your local community, you were fond of borrowing items from the young men and women who just opened little stores and were still trying to find their feet in business. When any of them refused to give you anything because of the bills you accumulated, you teamed up with tax collectors to put them out of business. Where did you think they were getting the money to buy the items you kept taking without paying? Why did you team up with tax collectors who always collected more than they were supposed to? Those who do that will render account when they get over here and those who collaborate with them in killing people who are trying to survive will equally render accounts. (*Common Man tries to say something*) I know what you want to say. My master is not against the collection of taxes but it should not be done in a way that would cripple the person paying it nor should tax collection be used as a tool for revenge or punishment.

Common Man: I'm deeply sorry.

Messenger: You walked into the office of a young girl called Jasmine in Money Express Bank. She was not in when you walked into her office. She just stepped out to go and ease herself. Your eyes fell on some bank notes you found on her table. After peeping around, you saw that nobody was watching you and you grabbed the bank notes and slid them under the large garment you had on and walked out of her office and sat outside in the area meant for customers. She soon returned and discovered that the money on her table was gone. She raised an alarm but was instead accused of stealing the money and pretending to make people believe that it was missing. Jasmine pleaded with whoever must have taken the money to bring it back in exchange for her end of month salary. You just sat there like a stone and did not even feel sorry for her. She lost her job over that incident which she knew nothing about. Have I said anything which was out of place?

Common Man: (*Remains silent*)

Messenger: You might escape the vigilance of men down there but you cannot escape that of my Master. Nobody has and nobody will ever escape the vigilance of my master. That was not all…before you left that world below

170

your feet you turned yourself into a preacher and opened a prayer house. Were you really out to serve your creator and prepare people for His kingdom?

Common Man: (*Remains silent*)

Messenger: Well, it seems you want me to go ahead. You opened your prayer house not to serve my master and prepare people for my master's kingdom but you were motivated by your love for money. Your principal targets were the rich families and rich widows. You employed investigators to find out everything about their private lives and you used the information they brought back to you to convince the rich families and widows to extort money from them. You claimed the information about their private lives was sent to you in a vision by my master. Was that true?

Common Man: (*Remains silent*)

Messenger: You planned and paid some young men and women who were very good performers. Their task was to behave as real cripples and you would perform miracles after which they would become whole again. You invited TV cameras during such performances and the tapes were multiplied and sold in many places around the world. Thousands of gullible people who watched such tapes abandoned their houses of prayers and flocked to you with various kinds of problems. You charged a fee before you could see them and after paying, their problems were not solved. When my master was down there too, He performed miracles as well but asked those who witnessed him perform them not to tell anyone outside. My master did that because

He did not want any publicity and His miracles were genuine. Yours were not genuine and the filming and sale of tapes showing you performing was evidence that you were out only for business. That was not all….you teamed up with some of your religious business partners in neighbouring countries and organized deliverance sessions in which you still performed your miracle dramas. You convinced the congregation to contribute money which you would use in carrying out developmental projects in their communities. When they contributed the money and handed it to you, you disappeared into thin air and ran back to your country after compensating your co-organizers. You turned the house of prayer into a money-making institution. That was not supposed to be and any man who indulges in such horrendous acts must remember that they will have to render accounts some day. Because of your deeds, many people lost faith in the house of prayer and eventually their only chance of getting into my master's kingdom. Your disciples are now more than double in the world and they are leading thousands of people astray. Whatever the case, they are deceiving their followers and themselves. They cannot deceive my master because He alone knows who serve him truly. So far, have I said anything which is out of place?

Common Man: (*With tears streaming down his face*) No.

Messenger: Good. You got involved in very unhealthy relationships with married women, widows and young girls in your congregation. You called them molecules. You soon discovered that you had a deadly and infectious disease which you picked up from one of your numerous concubines. "I cannot die alone. I will infect as many people as possible

172

before I die." Those were your exact words and you executed them to the latter. You infected mostly young girls and many of them are presently down there suffering from the disease. Some of them are not aware that they have been infected and are spreading the disease further. Where did you keep your conscience? That was the first court my master made and endowed every man with. It is the voice of my master within you. You were supposed to listen to that voice within you before taking any action. Did you do that? You went as far as dating the wife of your best friend Marcus. As soon as he discovered what was going on, he first of all came to you and pleaded with you to leave his wife alone. You did not do it. Out of anger and frustration, he decided to date your own wife in retaliation. The day you learnt of it, you picked your pistol and hunted for your friend all over the city to kill him. He fled to another town. But after a year, he realized that it was stupid for him to have responded to evil by doing evil and came to you to ask for your forgiveness. But you refused to forgive him and told him that no forgiveness was ever going to come from you while at the same time forgetting that you are the one who started dating his wife. "Do unto others what you would want others to do unto you. Where did you keep my master's commandment on love for your neighbour and the law forbidding you from coveting his wife?

Common Man: If I am here because I did not forgive my friend, I have now forgiven him.

Messenger: Forgiving him now is too late. All forgiveness and making of amends must be made down there before you leave that world. Because you refused to forgive your friend, my master could also not forgive you. If you want to be forgiven, you must forgive and accept forgiveness from others and then, my master who is all merciful will also forgive you. But it must be done only down there and not here. (*Pauses for a while*) We have not talked about all the unhealthy things you did. But let me draw your attention to one thing; you were looking for money all your life and even when you found some, it never stood in your hands. Do you know why? It is because each man was condemned to eat only from the sweat of his personal labour and not the labour of others. All the money you had could not remain in your hands because you used unorthodox means to acquire it. That is the fate for all ill gotten wealth. It goes to wastage. You should not expect good to come out of something acquired through evil means. Did you ask me to tell you that this is not the place you were warned about by the preachers? I'm sorry it is. This place is the reward for all those who refused to listen to the inner voices in them and refused to do the right things.

Common Man: (*Rolls on the ground crying*) Help me---help me---help me. I did not know that what I was doing was serious enough to lead me here. Please help me--- help me.

Messenger: I wish I could help you. The begging for help and repentance must be done before you cross that bar which separates this world from that one you've just come from. Now, it is too late. I just had to make you see clearly why you are here. Your landing here is very hurting to my master. It hurts more than you could ever imagine. There are others crowded in one of those rooms there. You can go and join them if you want.

(*Common Man prefers to be alone. Messenger exits*)

Scene 2: A short while later. A trumpet sounds and everybody has to assemble in the yard. The old comers take advantage of the assembly to acquaint themselves with Common Man. Messenger cannot be spotted.

William: (*To Common Man who is still crying*) you came here and you did not even come to see us? When did you come?

Common Man: Just a while ago. I can't believe I've ended up here. I was seriously warned about this place but I did nothing to avoid it.

William: It was the same thing with us. We all wanted and dreamed of (*pointing*) that golden city over there. But we did nothing to get there. You know, it's like desperately wanting something but doing nothing to obtain it.

Sandi: We all had nervous breakdowns when we came face to face with the reality of this place. If you are crying, it is just normal. But one thing you must know is that crying will do you no good. You are in here to stay for eternity. The earlier you get used to it, the better for you.

William: (To Sandi) indeed, you have a very strange way of consoling someone.

Sandi: What consolation can one really get in a place like this one? We are all doomed. Have I said anything to him which is not true? I just feel that the earlier he gets used to it, the better for him.

Common Man: Is there nothing that we can do for ourselves?

William: Do you mean to get out of here? Don't even think about it. If there was something we could do, we would have done it already. Sorry, you just have to adapt to the new situation.

Common Man: (*Sobs again*) I can't believe this has happened to me.

William: Cry a little if that will give you some relief. We are assembled here to get a last word from the messenger. After saying what he wants to say, he will probably ask all of us to move inland. There, you will realize that it is even hotter than this place. So, just be prepared.

Scene 3: In the yard. Messenger appears to deliver his sermon.

Messenger: There was a preacher called Kingston who worked in a small town called Victoria Bay. He did what he thought was his utmost best and there came a time when he had to go on transfer. Members of his congregation decided to organize a send-off ceremony for him. During the occasion, many speeches were made. What was said was so touching to the extent that the preacher wished the transfer never came. But there was an old woman who burst into tears after listening to all the good things that were said about the preacher.

"All these people have said so many good things about you but I would like to tell you that they are deceiving you. I will tell you what they say about you. Some of them say that you are very lazy and do not take adequate time to prepare your sermons. Others say that they don't like the way young girls and married women frequent your residence. So if you go to that new station, correct those aspects to be a better person," she said.

That is what happens with eulogies and there were many of such eulogies when you all left that world-check this sentence. It is not clear what you're trying to say. Anyone who listened to them left your burial grounds believing that you would be seated by my master's side by now. But those eulogies remained what they were. That is, they lacked touch with reality and most important facts concerning the lives you led, down there were left out. They equally collected money to offer many prayer intentions for you. But all that was in vain because the decision on where to go thereafter rested only in your hands. The actions of those still living could not in anyway influence the judgment of my master because He knows all the facts and sees right into the heart and soul of every man. While down there, you did your jobs as if life started and ended with you. You spent most of your time drawing up time tables forgetting one thing....death. You forgot that you were not masters of your destinies. You forgot that you were not the ones to choose when you die. You let your love for power push you to deny my master. You let your love for money push you to dishonour my master. You extorted and looted billions from people and the state forgetting to know that the size of your stomach could never increase. You let your intelligence or knowledge push you to question the existence of my master. You let your love for worldly pleasures push you to disobey my master. You had to know that you were just clay in the hands of a potter who did with you whatever He pleased. He made you and blessed you with positions which you had to use in making yourselves worthy for that kingdom (*pointing*) over there by serving humanity. He created everything you saw, enjoyed and loved. He asked to be master over them and that was what you were supposed to do. He never asked you to become a slave to what He created. In the days of old, my master performed miracles as well as spoke to man directly. When He came down there and left, that direct interaction ended. My master decided to intervene in the lives of humans indirectly through fellow humans. That is, the medical doctor is continuing with the healing mission, the president with the serving mission, the preacher with the preparation for the kingdom to come mission, the uniform officer with the defending and protecting mission, the farmer with the feeding mission, the lawyer with the justice seeking mission etc. You were supposed to continue with my master's miracles. There is no better way of serving and honouring my master than through the job and position you occupy. But you instead spent your time making those you had to serve feel how important you were, how powerful you were and how unique you were…. You saw them as tools or customers whose job was only to provide you with the money you needed…. you saw them as enemies because they were poor, looked different, inferior, uncivilized, belonged to another religion or were political opponents. Indeed, there were physical differences between you in terms of skin colour, ethnic background and differences in languages spoken. But my master took care of that my instituting one language which was a language of action….a language which had no words…. A language which every man understood….and it was the language of Love and service. Where could you better exercise it than in your work places or positions of responsibility that you occupied? My master tried to stop you in different ways and even when you were about to die, He still accorded you some time to make amends. Most people whose paths are straight do not spend much time on their dying beds. On the other hand most of those whose paths are not straight spend longer times on their sick beds. It is my master who accords that time for them to make straight their paths and also to teach the living a lesson. That is to say that you were all supposed to learn from what happened to those who were about to depart from that world before you. He accorded all of you here time to straighten your paths. Two minutes is enough time for anyone to straighten his or her path. But my master gave more than that to each and everyone of you. Sandi, when you strapped those explosives round your waist and blew yourself up with hundreds of others in that prayer house, you did not die immediately. You died seven minutes later. Within those seven minutes, you could have made your path straight with humanity and your creator. But you didn't. You instead used the time dreaming of a crown and virgins. As for you Stone, you were given months to make amends for the terrible things you did to your brothers and my master. Instead of doing just that, you wasted all the time wishing that your illness would disappear so that you could go back to what you knew best….hurting your brothers and making more money. As for you Carlos, the missile did not catapult you here instantly. You were badly wounded but you were rushed to the hospital where you spent three days. Though unconscious, you kept pleading with the doctor to save your life against a huge amount of money as reward. You also kept thinking of all the money you kept in foreign banks until time passed you by. William, you wasted your own time feeling too big to apologize because you thought that your reputation would be tarnished. You were equally regretting that life could not be longer. As regards you Cain, you were given three hours which you used regretting the losses you were incurring as you laid on your death bed. You were all given a last chance. You failed to use it. Now, you are all faced with the bitter reality. You were long told and now know that the life down there is a life of vanity. But it does not cancel the fact that the life of bliss thereafter must be prepared from down there. The fact that the life of man down there is very short should have been a reminder that you ought to listen to the inner voice in you before taking any action in order not to waste the short time you had in doing dishonourable things that would displease my master and land you here. By living a life of selfishness, greed, lust, envy, crime, you were preparing yourselves for this place though some of you were quick to point out that no man in his normal senses would choose this place. That place over there is meant only for people who have made amends and are worthy. That is why the road to get there is narrow, rough and difficult. Seconds were enough for each and everyone of you to make a difference and avoid this place but you refused to take advantage of them because you still had your eyes on the things of that world. Now that all your doubts have been cleared, it is time for you to move inland.

They all wail

Curtain

The End